D0301911

HELP!
I'M AN
ALIEN

JO FRANKLIN

Illustrated
by Aaron Blecha

troika books

For Eleanor and Cedric

First published in the UK by TROIKA BOOKS
Well House, Green Lane, Ardleigh CO7 7PD, UK
www.troikabooks.com

First published 2016

Text copyright © Jo Franklin 2016
Illustrations copyright © Aaron Blecha 2016

The moral rights of the author and illustrator have been asserted
All rights reserved

A CIP catalogue record for this book is available
from the British Library

ISBN 978-1-909991-29-3

1 2 3 4 5 6 7 8 9 10

Printed in Poland

1

Things You Need to Know About My Family

I have NOTHING in common with my family.

Mum and Dad met on a nudist beach in Tenerife. These days they are only nudists in the shower. I found this out by accident when Dad had forgotten to lock the bathroom door and I didn't notice the sound of running water and . . .

I bought Dad a mega strength padlock for Christmas.

My incredibly annoying older sister Jessie has a Random Mood Generator. She's constantly on shuffle but her favourite tracks are:

When Mum lost her wedding ring she found it using a metal detector. It was in my baby brother Timmy's body. Mum had to dig through all his nappies until she found it. She still wears it. Gross.

We live at 26 Beechwood Road but Dad thinks 26 is boring so he renamed our house and stuck a sign on the front. He thinks 'Konnichiwa' (hello in Japanese) is cool. He is wrong.

No one in my family knows my name. They call me Bod, short for Oddbod, but I happen to know my name is Daniel Kendal.

2

The Big Fat Family Secret

I like to eat breakfast on my own before going to school. It's safer that way and quieter. Every day I eat four Weetabix stacked like two double decker buses parked next to each other. I need the calories to feed my growing legs which are very long and very hungry. But today I hadn't finished eating when Jessie came in to annoy me.

'What is it with you and those freaky long legs, Oddbod?' Jessie said, waving her hair straighteners around like a pair of manic chopsticks.

'There's nothing wrong with my legs.' I grabbed the cereal packets and built a wall across the kitchen table. I was unarmed.

'They're weird and I don't want them anywhere

near me.' Jessie snapped her straighteners at my feet.

I pulled my legs back to my side of the table. No way was I letting her grab me with the super-heated jaws. I was already too tall for my age – I didn't need to be covered with stinky burnt hair as well.

'I don't even know what you're doing living in this house,' she said.

'I'm your brother.'

'You reckon?' Jessie pushed the cereal packets off the table and thrust her face at me.

I had a clear view up her nose. I'm not sure how Jessie got those hair straighteners up there without burning her nostrils, but the hair in my sister's nose was already straight.

'Wanna know the family secret?' she said. 'The one about you?'

'There's no secrets in this family,' I said, quoting one of Mum's favourite sayings.

'No secrets?' Jessie said. 'Are you sure about that?'

She was right and Mum was wrong. There are loads of secrets in our family and I know some of them.

My Top 5 Secrets of the Kendal Family

1. Mum says she's given up chocolate but I found a massive bar of Dairy Milk behind the microwave and the bar keeps getting smaller.

2. Timmy knows three rude words. I taught them to him last week.

3. Jessie had a puff on a cigarette at Uncle Jimmy's 40th birthday party and then she was sick. (Serves her right.)

4. Dad told Mum he was cutting Mrs Jenkins' hedge last week, but actually he was fixing Miss Duffy's car. Dad calls Miss Duffy 'Carol'. Mum calls her 'Killer Heels'.

5. I'm getting a new bike for Christmas. That's a secret I'm not supposed to know but there's a page ripped out of the Argos catalogue. I hope Mum orders the right bike because I hate pink.

There are loads of secrets in my family, but I don't think the big fat family secret Jessie was referring to was my new bike.

Jessie's Random Mood Generator was stuck on:

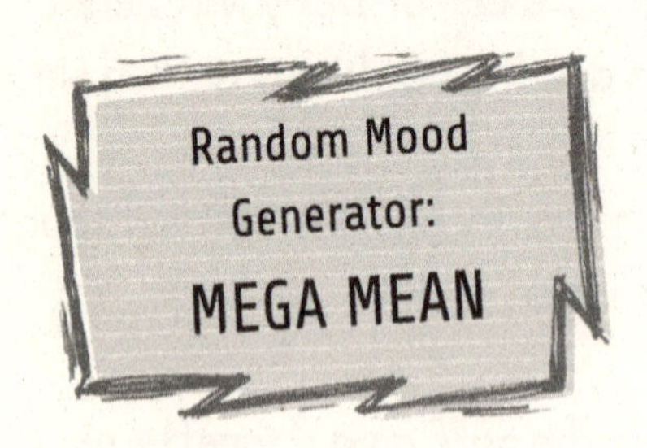

'You're not really my brother,' she hissed.

An icy chill of doom crept up my back and wrapped itself around my neck.

'You're an alien, abandoned on Earth by your alien parents.' She snapped her straighteners at me.

'Dad didn't want you.' *Snap.*

'I didn't want you.' *Snap.*

'But Mum felt sorry for you. And now we're stuck with you.' She whacked her stupid straighteners around my head as she got up to leave.

'Why don't you take your alien legs and go back where you came from? And you can take Serena Blake with you.'

'Serena Blake?' I said. 'Who's that?'

'A nutter in my year. See ya later, alien boy.' Jessie threw a crust of toast at me and stormed out.

What did she mean? Aliens didn't exist. Except in movies, and those aliens had tentacles, crazy black eyeballs or telescopic necks.

I wasn't like that. I was normal. Well, not exactly normal, but I was convinced I was human.

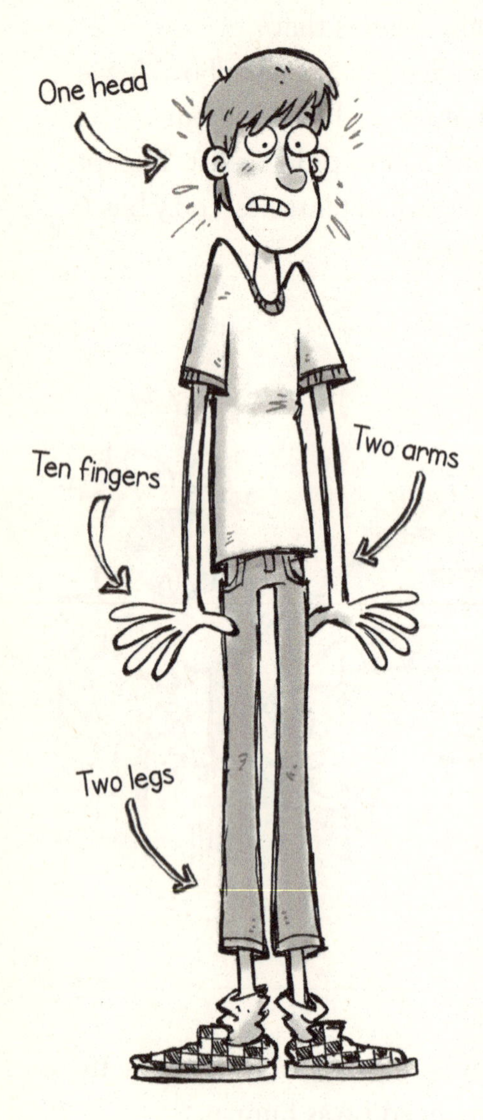

5 Reasons Why I Must Be Human

1. My blood is red. When Timmy had a tantrum and bit my leg, my blood dripped onto the carpet. It left a reddish-brown stain. It did NOT burn a hole through to the floorboards. Human blood, not alien.

2. I have the normal human number of legs, arms and heads.

3. I've never been to outer space. I don't have the right passport.

4. Aliens speak weird languages. I speak English and Swearing but I only say the bad stuff when I'm really angry and there are no adults around.

5. Aliens only have one emotion: SEEK AND DESTROY. I have the full range of human emotions and right now the one on top is PANIC.

I was a hundred per cent human – so what did Jessie mean? She said I wasn't really her brother.

A rock of doom smashed me in the stomach.

Was she trying to tell me I was adopted?

3

The Problem With Photographs

I was still wondering who I was when Timmy charged in and pointed at me.

'Bod. Bod. No good,' he said.

'Thanks, buddy, I'm beginning to realise that.' I slumped on the chair, the rock of doom so heavy I couldn't stand.

'Bod. Bod.' Timmy bashed his fists on my knees. I held his pudgy hands and looked at him closely. Then I thought about every other member of my family and what they looked like.

There was something very peculiar going on and I'd never noticed it before.

This is my analysis:

	Eyes	Hair	Height
Timmy	Baby blue	Blond, with Weetabix	Toddler
Jessie	Blue (evil)	Blond, with hair gunk	Teen plus heels
Mum	Blue (normal)	Blond, with help from hairdresser	Normal plus heels
Dad	Blue (bloodshot)	Missing	Shorter than Mum
Me	Mud brown	Curly Wurly brown	Taller than everyone else in my family, my school and my street

This is my conclusion: I don't have a single strand of DNA in common with any of my so-called family.

When Mum and Dad came into the kitchen, all I could do was stare. How come I'd never noticed it before? I look nothing like them.

'Jessie gone to school, Bod?' Mum said as she strapped Timmy into his high chair.

'Lego!' Timmy shouted.

'She told me I'm not her brother,' I said.

'Oh!' Mum and Dad said at exactly the same time, as if they were telepathic. It's perfectly normal for best friends to be telepathic, but it's totally weird between husband and wife, particularly when they are being telepathic about me. I think they were both freaking out at exactly the same moment because the truth about my misfit DNA was no longer a secret.

'Lego!' Timmy banged his fists down on the tray of his high chair.

'Why did Jessie say that?' I said. 'I want to know the truth.'

'Don't take any notice of Jessie.' Dad picked up the toaster and turned it upside down. He was pretending the bread was stuck inside but his bread was still sitting on his plate. I reckon Dad was studying the guts of the toaster as a way of avoiding my question.

'Where did I come from, Mum?' I said.

'It all starts with a little egg and a little seed, but I haven't got time for this now, Bod.' Mum grabbed a cereal bowl and slammed it on the table. Her ears had gone bright red, as if she was embarrassed about something. And I reckoned that embarrassing thing was the fact that I was adopted.

'I know about the egg and the seed, but that's not what I'm talking about.' I kicked the chair. 'I mean ME!'

'Can we talk about this later?' Mum didn't bother looking up. 'Timmy, it's breakfast time. No Lego at the table.'

'Lego!' Timmy shouted.

'Weetabix!' Mum shouted back.

Timmy prefers toast. But Mum won't give it to him since I taught him to play toast Frisbee and a rogue piece stuck to her bum. It could have saved her a trip to the sandwich shop at lunchtime, only a dog found it before she did and nearly ripped her skirt off on the way to work.

Toast Frisbee is now banned in this house.

'How did I come into this family?' I said.

Dad cleared his throat and stared out of the window.

'Open wide, Timmy,' Mum said as she tried to push the spoon into Timmy's mouth.

'Any more butter?' Dad said.

'In the fridge,' Mum said.

I felt exactly like that piece of Frisbee toast. Lonely and stuck somewhere I didn't belong.

Dad was too busy avoiding the little egg/little seed talk to listen to me.

Mum was too busy looking after Timmy.

My parents didn't want to speak to me, their maybe-adopted son. I needed hard evidence – *then* they'd have to tell me the truth.

I grabbed my school bag and made out I was leaving the house. But I sneaked into the sitting room instead. The family photo albums were on the bottom shelf of the bookcase.

Every year on 31 December, Mum goes through all the photos she has taken that year and picks out the best ones to make a photo album. She's really particular about it. She says she likes to reflect on the year and remember all the really important things that have happened to us. She takes loads of photos all year, but only the best ones go in the album.

In among the photos she sticks other scraps. Old cinema tickets, flyers from museums we have visited, newspaper articles about family members.

I pulled out the album for the year I was born. I'd never looked at Mum's photos before. I didn't need to be reminded what an oddbod freak I've been for ten years. I flicked through the pages. My birthday is in April, so I should have found myself a quarter of the way through the album.

Photos I Found

- Jessie in a Snow White outfit trampling over seven dwarfs
- Jessie ripping a teddy's arms off. (She hasn't changed.)
- Jessie with no clothes on at the beach.

I turned the page quickly. Jessie was only four in the photo and I hadn't even been born, but I didn't need to see her training to be a nudist.

After that the pages were completely blank.

In the year I was supposed to have been born, Mum's photo album was empty. There were no photos of me as a baby.

The rock of doom had left me. Instead I felt empty.

Four Weetabix weren't enough to fill the howling

emptiness of not being a true member of the family.

I slapped the blank book shut. A scrap of paper flew out between the pages and floated to the floor. One of Mum's old newspaper cuttings. Probably something about Jessie winning the most beautiful baby competition or how Grandad had won a rosette for his prize marrow. I didn't need to read about their mega achievements but I didn't know where the scrap came from so I shoved it in my pocket.

I grabbed the next album off the shelf and flipped it open.

Jessie's first school photo. Jessie dressed as a pirate with a gap in her teeth.

I flipped the page.

At last, a picture of me. I was standing by the kitchen table with my hands in the air.

Mum had written *I can walk!* underneath.

In the photo I wasn't a baby. I was already a toddler.

I kept turning the pages. There I was:

- Me riding my push along car (knees up to my chin).

• Me on Dad's bike (in a child seat on the back, my long legs dragging in the dirt).

• Me at the seaside (using a Mr Whippy ice cream cone as suntan cream while the rest of the family eat theirs).

In every photo I was getting older and taller.

The next album was the same. They were all chock full of photos of Jessie and me growing up. The albums for the last two years included pictures of Timmy.

Jessie and Timmy looked like twins with an age gap. Blond hair, blue eyes, always smiling. I was always scowling, standing separately.

I can't smile for photos and my hair is different from theirs. I look like a neighbour dragged along for a Kendal family outing.

There was absolutely no photographic record of Baby Daniel – me. In a family where photos are taken all the time, that could only mean one thing.

I wasn't part of this family when I was a baby. I was born somewhere else.

I must have been adopted.

4

The Truth About Me and My Life

I left the house to walk to school. Only I couldn't walk, I trudged. The photographic truth weighed me down so I couldn't lift my feet off the pavement. I wasn't a true Kendal.

'Nice socks!' the postman said.

I looked down at my ankles to see what he was on about. I was wearing Snoopy socks.

I like to get dressed in the dark. That way I don't have to look at myself. Who wants to be reminded that they're too-tall-to-be-normal first thing in the morning? Unfortunately, today's socks were given to me by Jessie as a sick Christmas joke.

A builder wolf-whistled from the top of some high scaffolding.

'Nice socks!' he shouted.

I was going to be mullered when I got to school. Novelty socks are *not* cool. Who is Snoopy anyway? I ducked behind a wheelie bin and raided my school bag for a black felt tip. I coloured in Snoopy so that it looked like I was wearing black socks under my too-short jeans. Only the black pen rubbed off onto my skin so it looked like I hadn't washed for a week. Luckily the felt pen didn't smell so I reckoned no one would notice.

If Mum had bought me trousers that fitted, the whole 'nice socks' thing would go away. But obviously I wasn't as important to her as her other kids, the ones she'd given birth to.

I managed to get into my classroom without any more 'Nice Socks' comments, thanks to my fantastic black felt pen. Freddo was already there.

The Ideal Best Friend	Freddo, My Best Friend
Cool dude	Crisp addict
Sharp dresser	Fart master
Smart / clever / funny	Put-down king

'I've got a good one for you today, Dan my man,' Freddo said. 'Ready for the Toxic Samurai?'

Freddo is always trying to impress me with his extreme personal habits. Last week it was the world's biggest bogey. Only by the time he brought it into school, it had dried out and looked more like a mini rubber band than a snot-busting record breaker.

'Stand back,' he said. 'I could accidently kill you.'

He tensed his body and raised his hands in a defensive kung fu position. He scowled and went cross eyed.

'Get on with it, mate,' I said. 'Mr Pitdown's going to walk in any minute.' Mr Pitdown is our class teacher. He's not impressed by Freddo's extreme personal habits.

Freddo hopped up and down on one leg and lashed out with the other, spinning his whole body round. As he whizzed past he let rip an enormous fart.

Pppppffffffftttttt!

Totally immersed in his stinking whirlwind, his foot caught under a chair, throwing it into the air. It sailed over his head towards a huddle of girls who were too busy whispering and giggling to notice.

'Watch out!' Rooners, the captain of the Football Gang, shouted as he launched himself at the girls, shoving them out of the way.

The flying chair rebounded off the wall and flew into the centre of the room. The legs became tangled in a piece of string suspending a globe of the world from the ceiling. The world and the chair came crashing down onto Mr Pitdown's desk.

'How's that?' Freddo panted.

'Urghh!'

'Open the window!'

'Gross!' the rest of the class said.

'Toxic,' I said, holding my nose. I was far too familiar with the smell of Freddo's guts to risk breathing without taking precautions. I gave him the thumbs up with my free hand.

'Brilliant!' Freddo said as he balled his early-morning crisp packet and threw it in the bin. 'Class photo! I forgot my comb,' he said. 'Do you think anyone will notice?' He slid his crisp-encrusted fingers through his hair.

'Nah,' I said. 'Looks normal.'

Freddo wasn't bothered about stuff like washing his hair. I could see a few crisp crumbs in amongst the grease but I didn't say anything in case he tried to get rid of them and the teachers thought he was picking out nits. I didn't want Freddo to be sent home from school with a nit letter today. I had important adoption stuff to discuss with him.

'Great T-shirt by the way,' he said and slapped me on the shoulder.

T-shirt? I'd been so hung up on the sock problem, I'd forgotten I was wearing one of Dad's T-shirts. All my T-shirts were way too small for me so I'd grabbed the nearest thing from the airing cupboard. I looked down at my chest. The T-shirt I was wearing had *World's Number 1 Dad* printed across it.

'I'm not ready to be a father yet,' I said.

'Try this one for size.' Freddo pulled a brand new T-shirt out of his school bag. 'Dad's got new stock in.'

'Thanks.' I ripped the T-shirt out of its wrapper. Freddo has got some disgusting personal habits but is THE best friend in the world. Freddo's dad runs a market stall and Freddo has inherited his knack for always having exactly the right thing at the right time. And luckily for me Freddo likes to share.

Rooners shouted something about Mr Pitdown wanting us to go to the hall for the photo.

'Come on. The evil photographer awaits.' My Number 1 best friend shoved the shirt into my hands, let rip another evil fart and disappeared into the corridor.

I dashed into the toilets to get changed. Gordon, my second best friend, stood in front of the mirror adjusting his tie.

Freddo thinks Gordon may be a very short adult spy disguised as a kid. I don't agree. I think Gordon is just a geek with terrible taste in clothes. He wears full school uniform, including a blazer, which is pretty sad as our school doesn't have a uniform. But Freddo and I let him hang out with us because he's

got loads of cool gadgets like a microdot camera, a tie-pin microphone and night-vision goggles. He lets us look at them if we've washed our hands.

Gordon also has a nasty habit of speaking the truth, the whole truth and nothing but the truth. So I don't think he can be a spy because spies have to be very good at keeping secrets.

'Good morning,' Gordon said.

'Nightmare,' I said.

I pulled on the new T-shirt, and before I had a chance to look at myself in the mirror, the door to the corridor flew open and our class teacher came in.

'Gordon. Daniel. Hall, now!' Mr Pitdown shouted.

Gordon took one more look in the mirror and flicked an invisible speck off his blazer.

'Very smart.' Mr Pitdown nodded as Gordon left the room.

My teacher looked me up and down and muttered something under his breath.

I couldn't hear properly but it was something like, 'Where did *that* come from?' He was talking about me, of course.

I wasn't the World's Number 1 Dad any more but even Mr Pitdown, the weirdest teacher at school, could see I didn't fit in.

5

Photographs - Who Needs Them?

My class were already in the hall for the class photo. They sat on tiers of chairs so that everyone's head was roughly in line with the other kids on their row. For some reason when I walked in they all started laughing.

I took the only empty seat. Front row, far left. Freddo sat somewhere in the middle, a million miles away from me. Gordon sat at the other end of my row.

'Hey you! The abnormally tall one with the T-shirt!' the photographer shouted. 'Back row, please. You're ruining the shot.'

I slouched down in the seat, trying to make my abnormality smaller. I didn't know why he was picking on me. I wasn't the only kid wearing a T-shirt.

'Back row!' The photographer waved a laser pointer at me. I thought I was about to be assassinated so I shuffled round to the back of the scaffolding.

'I'm not sure I can . . .' I looked up at the empty seat on the back row. 'That's high.'

'Daniel, back row. Now!' Mr Pitdown bellowed.

The whole class groaned as I clambered up the steps to join the boys way up on the back row. I swear those steps were made of jelly or something because the higher I climbed, the more they wobbled.

By the time I was at the top, the room was one great shimmering hologram. Nothing solid. Nothing real. I grabbed hold of something to steady myself. Then something screamed, and when I looked down I realised I had my hands full of girls' hair.

'Daniel, leave Susan Albright alone!' Mr Pitdown shouted.

The class burst out laughing.

'It's no good. Your head is now way out.' The photographer waved his red dot all over my face as if he was trying to scribble me out. 'Come and lie down at the front.' He drew a red laser line across the feet of the front row.

The minute my feet touched the floor the wobbly

feeling in my guts was replaced with a heavy feeling of doom. Lying at the feet of my class was a bad idea.

I kept hoping Freddo would do something to rescue me. But the best friend telepathy can't have been working. Freddo just grinned, stroked his top lip (which is our code for 'Mr Pitdown is a moron') and gave me the thumbs up.

Gordon sat at the end of the front row. I raised an eyebrow, hoping for a bit of solidarity, but he ignored me. His eyes were focused on the camera, ready to have his photo taken. Gordon always does exactly as he's told.

I lay down, with a class full of Year 6 feet a few centimetres away. I put my head in front of Gordon's feet. He was the only person I could trust not to kick me. Gordon doesn't do touching.

'What is that on your legs?' Mr Pitdown said.

My trousers had hitched up so everyone could see the dirty felt-tip marks on my leg.

'Please, sir, I can't sit here,' the girl sitting by my ankles said. 'I've got my best shoes on and my mum will kill me if I get them ruined.' She pulled her shoes up and hid them under her skirt.

'Daniel Kendal!' Mr Pitdown roared like Godzilla.

'You are ruining the photo on purpose. Out in the corridor, now! And take your rubbish with you.' He pointed at a scrap of newspaper on the floor.

I snatched up the piece of rubbish and went out into the corridor. I slammed the door shut so I didn't have to hear the sadist photographer telling everyone to say 'Cheese' ten thousand times.

There were no seats in the corridor so I sat on the floor, rested my head against the wall and stared at my reflection in the shiny metal bin shoved in the corner. That's when I saw what was on the T-shirt Freddo had given me.

'Thanks, Freddo!'

No wonder Mr Pitdown didn't like me. There was no way he was going to let me be in the school photo wearing that T-shirt. *And* he made me pick up someone else's rubbish as a punishment. I was about to ball the scrap of paper I'd picked up from the floor to slamdunk it in the rubbish bin when I realised it wasn't someone else's rubbish after all. It was the newspaper cutting that had fallen out of Mum's photo album. I'd shoved it into my pocket at home without looking at it and it must have fallen out when I was being humiliated at the feet of my classmates. I smoothed out the paper to see what had been so important for Mum to keep in amongst the family photos. It was dated 25 April. My birthday.

METEOR CRASHES TO EARTH IN PARK

Police have been inundated by reports of a falling star crashing to Earth in local Park Hill Fields.

Police are mystified by a large crater that has appeared in the middle of the football pitch, but no evidence of the meteor itself has been found. Fragments of something from outer space may have been removed by meteor hunters.

The Ministry of Defence say that it is highly unlikely to have been an alien spaceship crash-landing on Earth.

It happened on my birthday. Mum kept the newspaper cutting because it was about me.

My head buzzed with a billion thoughts. I tried to line them up so they made sense.

My birthday.

↓

Alien spaceship landed.

↓

Baby alien inside.

↓

Mum and Dad pulled alien baby from crashed ship.

↓

Dad put remains of spaceship in a skip.

↓

Mum took alien baby (me!) home.

↓

They decided to keep me.

↓

Baby alien becomes Daniel Kendal.

↓

Mum keeps newspaper clipping to remind her
of how I came to be in this world.

Jessie was right.

I wasn't just adopted.

I was an alien.

No wonder I didn't fit in. No wonder they didn't want me in the class photo. I'd tried being human for ten years but I'd been wasting my time. A shiver went up and down my extra-long body as my brain took in the truth. I was a different species. Maybe even a superior race. One that didn't belong on Earth.

I was the ultimate misfit.

I came from another planet.

A real live extra-terrestrial.

I was still digesting this awesome fact when Mr Pitdown called me back into the hall. 'Individual portraits now, Daniel. I hope you are going to behave.'

I nodded. My inner alien wanted to tell him I hadn't done anything wrong. Ten years of human experience told me not to bother arguing.

I joined the back of the line.

'These portraits are going to be very important,' Mr Pitdown said, addressing the whole class. 'We are going to create a Wall of Wonders in the classroom.'

'What's that, sir?' Susan Albright asked.

'I'm going to pin up all your portraits on the classroom wall and whenever you do a particularly good piece of work or are picked for the school football team, I will post a commendation under your picture.' Mr Pitdown rolled the tip of his moustache between his finger and thumb. 'In addition, you can add personal messages to your friends' pictures. At the end of the year, each member of the class will have a full memento of their last year at this school.'

'Cool!' The Football Gang slapped each other's hands and whooped.

The girls huddled in groups and whispered.

I didn't want to have my photo taken with these humans. I didn't need anything that reminded me of my last year at human junior school. I had nothing in common with them. As I edged closer to the photographer, an epic idea started forming in my head. The empty feeling in my stomach changed into a warm, fuzzy feeling. A feeling of certainty. A feeling of strength. At last, I knew who I was.

I plonked myself on the chair in front of the camera.

'Too tall!' the photographer said.

'You could adjust your tripod,' I said.

'I really need individual pictures of the whole class,' Mr Pitdown said. 'Do as you are told, Daniel, just kneel down.' He pointed to a spot on the floor.

The whole class sniggered. Freddo shoved his hand up his jumper and pumped his elbow up and down while he armpit-farted the tune of *Mission: Impossible*.

Humans enjoy humiliating species from other planets. Even human best friends.

I sank to my knees.

'Smile!' the photographer said.

I pulled my most demented alien face and made a decision.

Click! The photographer took the shot.

Mum could stick the photo in her album if she wanted to, but that was going to be the last picture ever taken of me on Earth.

I didn't belong here. I needed to return to wherever I came from.

The alien known as Daniel Kendal was going home.

6

Assembling the Mission Team

'Are you crazy?' Freddo said at break time.

He's supposed to be my best friend, but when I told him my earth-shattering news he didn't believe me.

'I'm an alien,' I said. 'It explains everything.'

'Like what?'

'Why everyone in class thinks I'm a weirdo.'

Freddo looked at me blankly.

'Even you think I'm abnormal, don't you?' I leant down and patted him on the head.

'You're tall, but I don't see how that makes you extra-terrestrial.

So I listed everything else I could think of.

My Family's Favourite Things	My Favourite Things
Tea	Chocolate malt milkshake with instant gravy sprinkles
Toast	Baked beans on Weetabix
Lying in the sun (sometimes naked)	Hiding in the dark (always fully dressed)
Football and other team games involving balls	Hanging out with the Fart Master and the Geek

Freddo looked at me as if I was the biggest saddo on the planet.

'Maybe your family don't like your chocolate malt combo because it's disgusting. I wouldn't eat it,' he said and stuffed a fistful of crisps in his mouth.

'That's because you're human and I'm not,' I said. 'I'm telling you, I don't fit into my family and I certainly don't fit in around here. I'm not even in the class photo. I must be from somewhere else. AND my favourite sweets are flying saucers, those weird sweets made of rice paper and filled with sherbet.'

'I've never seen you eat flying saucers,' Freddo said.

'I don't eat them because I want to fly in them,' I said. 'You believe in aliens, don't you?' I asked my second best friend.

Gordon the Geek was glued to his laptop as usual. He'd tied a string to it and hung it round his neck. It made him look like he was selling ice creams at the theatre. Gordon didn't like ice cream, but this was the best way he'd found for sucking up every bit of information from the internet into his brain.

'I'm an alien. Do you believe me?' I waved my hand in front of Gordon's face, being really careful not to touch him.

'Cosmic,' he replied, but he wasn't listening. He didn't look up and his fingers kept moving over the keys as we walked across the playground. Freddo and I have to guide him everywhere. We could lead him straight into an open manhole or the cracks of doom and he'd never know. But at least he'd die happy.

'If you are an alien, which planet are you from?' Freddo asked.

I didn't know the answer.

Freddo ripped open his empty crisp packet and licked up the grease and additives stuck to the inside.

He folded the wet plastic into a paper aeroplane but before he could fly it, the plastic had flopped open into a ripped crisp packet again.

He'd tried to make an aeroplane out of a crisp packet every day since the beginning of term. It never worked.

'Planet Kepler 22b.' Gordon looked up. His eyes blinked furiously as he adjusted to the big wide world rather than the eleven-inch virtual world he'd been glued to.

'Are you sure?' I said.

'Kepler 22b. Two point four times the size of Earth. Surface temperature twenty-two degrees centigrade. Six hundred light years away.'

'What's that in English?' Freddo gets annoyed with Gordon sometimes. Luckily Gordon doesn't notice and continues to hang out with us, otherwise I'd only have one friend on this planet.

'Approximately three thousand, six hundred trillion miles from Earth. It's the answer to global warming. When this planet explodes, that's where we're heading.' Gordon turned his laptop round and showed me a screen. It was a page from some scientific news service. It had a video showing what the scientist thought Kepler 22b looked like.

It was amazing. I'd never heard of Kepler 22b, but that planet was calling to me.

'So you mean there is a planet out there with aliens on it?' Freddo squinted at the screen.

'I don't suppose they consider themselves aliens when they're there.' Gordon opened another tab on his screen and clicked on an online dictionary. 'Alien – noun. Non-naturalised foreigner, a being from another world.

'Kepler 22b is home to them. They're not aliens there. Humans would be alien to the inhabitants of that planet.'

And to me.

When is an Alien Not an Alien?

I think I will be happy if I can get back to Kepler 22b but I do have a few burning questions that need answers:

Does chocolate exist on Kepler 22b?

What does an alien bike look like?

Is a high-five a suitable alien greeting?

It's really important that I fit in the minute I get there. I won't be an alien or a misfit or an oddbod. For once I'll be normal. I'll be a . . .

'What do you think the inhabitants of Kepler 22b call themselves?' I asked the mission crew while we queued for lunch.

'Chips, please,' Freddo said to the dinner lady.

'Keplerites?' I said. 'What d'you reckon, Gordon?'

Every day, Gordon the Geek lines up for lunch with Freddo and me. He rests his laptop and his briefcase on a tray and shoves it along the conveyor while we chat, but he never eats anything. He thinks school food is contaminated and a packed lunch is dangerous because it hasn't been kept in the fridge all morning.

'Kepler is the name of the telescope that spotted the planet,' Gordon said.

'So Kepler is a human word?' I asked.

Gordon looked at me over the top of his glasses like a cheesed-off but very intelligent professor. 'Yes. Kepler is a human word. There *are* only human words here because we don't know any aliens or how they speak.'

'You know me,' I said.

'But you weren't an alien until yesterday,' Freddo said and he rolled his eyeballs so far back into his head he must have been looking at his brain. If he had one.

'I know you,' Gordon said. 'But you were brought up by humans and speak human. English, actually. I guess you can call it a dialect of human speech.'

'Do you think the inhabitants of Kepler 22b have different languages?' A meteor of panic hit me hard in the stomach. 'What if I finally get to meet one of them and they come from North Kepler 22b and I came from South Kepler 22b and I can't understand a word they're saying?'

'Mr Kendal, do you speak any language other than English?' Gordon only calls me Mr Kendal when he's bored.

'No.'

'So if some Spanish girl walked in now and started chatting away, you wouldn't understand her. Right?' Gordon said.

'I'd understand every word,' Freddo smirked.

I turned my back on Freddo and slammed my tray onto the table. There are times when I want to take my best friend's head and shove it in the deep-fat fryer with his crisps and chips.

'I'd understand any kid if they pointed to the food and used sign language,' I said to Gordon.

'There you go,' said Gordon. 'You're going to have to make do with sign language *if* you ever meet anyone from Kepler 22b. Because you won't be able to understand them unless they speak English.'

Gordon was right. I was a moron. I only knew one language. I should have paid more attention in European Languages Week. It was all German,

French and Spanish, not Alien, but the more languages you know, the easier it is to understand a non-English speaker.

Remind me to sign up for Italian club.

Mr Pitdown printed out the portraits and created the Wall of Wonders over lunch. By the end of the day most of the portraits had personal messages added to them. Things like *BFF* and sparkly stickers on the girls' photos. *Greatest Goal Keeper* and *Cool Shirt* on the boys.

Someone wrote *Most snoggable mouth* under Freddo's photo. Freddo has amazing teeth. He eats too many crisps and he has some extremely disgusting personal habits, but his teeth are perfectly straight. There were other comments too:

The last one was in Freddo's handwriting. I'm not sure these were the sort of comments Mr Pitdown had in mind.

No one had written anything on my photo.

I tried to clean the marker pen off, but Mr Pitdown said not to bother. I suggested I took the picture home to see if Dad could clean it up. But he muttered something about 'Why does everything lead to bullying these days?' He needn't have worried. Aliens like me are used to that sort of thing. By the end of the day all the photos were totally covered in graffiti. Some of it was rude. Mr Pitdown took down the Year 6 Wall of Wonders and printed off fresh photos for everyone to take home. Except me. I guess he forgot. Either that or he decided that I didn't deserve one as I am only an alien.

8

I am a Long Way From Home

The alien persecution on Earth was getting me down. I needed to get back to Kepler 22b asap. But I couldn't do it on my own.

I invited my only friends round for a secret meeting.

Freddo, Gordon and I always hang out at my house. Gordon won't let us into his home because he doesn't like to have his personal space invaded – by aliens or humans. Freddo has so many brothers, cousins, uncles with girlfriends, babies and grandparents, we'd never get a moment on our own at his house.

Venue: Timmy's playhouse.

Address: Middle of Kendal family lawn
(back garden).

Good point: no one can overhear us. My bedroom has very thin walls.

Bad point: venue on the small side.

Timmy's playhouse is supposed to be a den for a single two year old, not three Year 6 boys – one with abnormally long alien legs, another with disgusting personal habits and another with a non-touching phobia of epic proportions and a laptop.

'Is it clean?' Gordon said as he bent down to peer through the tiny door.

The playhouse was empty except for Timmy's red chair. I'd scrubbed off a smear of strawberry jam and a dead Jaffa Cake before Gordon had arrived.

'One hundred per cent sterile,' I said.

Gordon zapped the playhouse inside and out with a variety of disinfectant sprays and wiped down Timmy's chair a hundred times before he sat on it. His knees nearly came up to his chin but there was just room for his laptop as long as he undid the string. There was no room to revive him if the string got knotted and strangled him. And anyway, mouth-to-mouth resuscitation would kill Gordon for sure.

Freddo bounded across the lawn hugging a huge plastic bag.

'Got something for you.' He thrust the bag into my arms.

It was a sack of flying saucers.

'Thanks,' I said.

'Open it, then,' Freddo said. 'Maybe if you eat enough, the sherbet will produce enough gas to lift you off this planet.'

I didn't want to admit to Freddo that I hadn't actually been truthful about flying saucers being my favourite sweet, but I put one in my mouth anyway. It tasted of paper. I bit down into the crisp shell and a blast of sherbet spread over my tongue. A saccharine fizz spread up my nose and made my eyes water.

'Epic!' I grinned, hoping I sounded convincing. Freddo was only trying to help.

Freddo shoved his hand into the bag and pulled out a fistful of rice-paper sweets. He shoved them in his mouth, chewed for a few seconds and then coughed the lot onto Dad's lawn.

'Gross!' he said. 'You *must* be from another planet if you like them.' Freddo stuck his finger in his mouth and prised out a wodge of stuck-together rice paper. He flicked the lot into the hedge.

'Hello?' A geeky voice came from the playhouse. 'The meeting is officially ten minutes late starting.'

'Stand back, I'm coming in.' Freddo shoved his right foot through the playhouse door.

'Before you do that,' I said, 'you need to swear.'

'No problem,' Freddo said and he spouted an impressive string of rude words. The final one sounded something like, 'Zakryxkekny!'

'Where did you get that one from?' I said.

'Made it up,' Freddo said. 'Sounds good, doesn't it?'

'Yeah, but I didn't mean that sort of swearing.' I took out a dictionary. It was the most official-looking book I could find. 'Stick your hand on that and read these words.' I'd written a solemn oath on a card for him.

'Are you serious?' Freddo laughed.

'You must swear or you're off the mission team.'

Freddo snorted, but he put his hand on the dictionary and chanted,

'I, Freddo, do solemnly promise that I will not fart . . .' Freddo choked on his words, '. . . in the meeting.'

'Thanks,' I said and put the card away.

The problem with Freddo is he's eaten so many crisps over the years he's rather large. The problem with me is I'm taller than the human inhabitants of this planet.

It took me and Freddo ten minutes to squeeze ourselves into the playhouse.

I stuck my legs out of the window so they didn't touch Gordon accidently.

Freddo sat in the doorway, his butt sticking out towards the house. Just in case.

'Consider me an early warning system,' he said. 'I'll let one off if anyone approaches.'

'No!' Gordon tried to get up but he couldn't move without touching us.

I tried to hit Freddo over the head with the dictionary but it was wedged between my elbow and my right ear.

'Only joking,' Freddo said. 'My buttocks are clenched. But get on with it, I can't hold it in forever. I had beans with my chips last night as we'd run out of ketchup.'

Remind me never to hold the mission meeting in Timmy's playhouse again. Also remind me to check out what Freddo had for tea before I invite him round next time.

I started the meeting by saying, 'All good missions need a mission statement. How about "I need to return to Kepler 22b"?'

'That's not a mission statement. That is your crazy dream,' Freddo said.

'To return the alien known as Daniel Kendal to Kepler 22b,' Gordon said.

'Nice one,' I said.

'Are you sure you're an alien?' Freddo asked. 'Maybe you're adopted.'

'Of course I'm adopted. I'm an alien, aren't I? My parents are not my parents, because they are human.'

'Maybe you are an adopted human from another human family.'

Freddo was really beginning to bug me. Why can't he accept me for what I am?

'I am not human. I am an alien. Jessie told me, and my parents have been trying to keep the secret from me forever. *That's* why I don't fit in here. And that's why I *need* to get back to my home planet.' The smell of Freddo's cheese-and-onion breath and his bad attitude were getting on my nerves. 'How am I going to get back to Kepler 22b?'

Freddo stuck his finger between his gum and his teeth and came out with another wad of soggy flying saucer. He rolled it between his finger and thumb.

'Don't . . .' But before I could complete the sentence he'd flicked the flying saucer/saliva combo at the ceiling.

Freddo winked.

I would have poked his stupid winking eye out if I could have reached over without touching Gordon.

'You're going to have to go into hibernation if you want to arrive on Kepler 22b alive.' Gordon looked up from his laptop, oblivious to the fact that a flying saucer time bomb infected with Freddo's germs hung five centimetres immediately above his head. His eyes wandered around in their sockets for a bit before fixing their gaze on me. 'It's so far away.'

I dragged my eyes away from the time bomb and tried to concentrate on what Gordon was saying.

'Hibernation? How do I do that?'

'Cryogenics. You'll need to be frozen alive.'

I didn't like the sound of it but I knew Gordon was right. The journey to Kepler 22b was a long one and I didn't want to be an old man when I arrived there. I wanted to be a normal Keplerite kid. To go to a school where I fitted in. I wanted to buy a Keplerite smart phone and maybe even start dating in a few years' time.

'So how does this cryogenic thing work?' I said.

Gordon took a couple of deep breaths. He opened his eyes wide, but the black pupils in the centre shrank down to tiny dots as he stared at me very intently.

'We're going to need a lot of ice.'

9

The Most Awesome Plan Ever

By the end of the meeting I knew exactly what I needed to do to get to Kepler 22b.

<u>MISSION STATEMENT</u>

To return the alien known as Daniel Kendal to Kepler 22b.

<u>PREPARATION AND TRAINING</u>

1. Test cryogenic survival, a.k.a. being frozen alive.
2. Find country with plans to relocate to Kepler 22b.

3. Raise cash for airfare to foreign country.

4. Get fit. Astronauts have to be in peak physical condition.

5. Pack stuff to take to new planet.
   - Handheld games console and charger
   - Backup handheld games console and charger
   - All games for games console and backup games console
   - 3 latest copies of *The Beano* to read while waiting for take off

6. Things to swap with Kepler kids to make friends:
   - Deadly Venomous Snake cards
   - Dinosaur stickers
   - Plastic yoyo and any other party-bag goodies

'With stuff like that I'm going to be really popular on Kepler 22b,' I said as I called the meeting to an end.

'What makes you think any kid wants a cheap yoyo that doesn't work? You'd be better off taking a MegaYo or a YoYammer,' Freddo said. 'Anyway, what happens to a yoyo in zero gravity?'

'It floats around like a helium balloon,' Gordon said.

'They have gravity on Kepler 22b. 'I was getting fed up with Freddo spoiling my plans. 'It's a planet, isn't it?' My voice was too loud for such a small space and Freddo doesn't like being shouted at. Especially by me.

'I'm out of here,' Freddo said. He wrapped his arm around his head and twisted his body in an attempt to leave the tiny playhouse head first.

I didn't know if it was Freddo's escape attempt or my shouting but I noticed the rice-paper time bomb was on the move. A ball bearing of mush was now dangling from the ceiling on a fine wet thread and the gap between it and the Geek's head was closing. There was no way I could smash it out of the way without Gordon seeing it. If he knew it was there, he would totally freak.

I needed Gordon. If he got contaminated, he'd leave the mission. Without Gordon I'd be stuck on Earth forever, but I couldn't reach the glob above his head. Freddo was ruining everything.

'They probably don't have yoyos on Kepler 22b,' I shouted at Freddo as he tried to wiggle free. 'The alien kids will have their own things to swap and as my Earth collectibles are so rare they'll give me loads of Keplerite stuff in return. My Black Mamba card is particularly awesome. It's worth a Keplerite smart phone on its own.'

Freddo grunted as he flung his body towards the grass outside. His legs flew up like a tarantula on *Strictly Come Dancing*. His heel caught the roof of the playhouse and with a screech of plastic it flew into the air, taking the wad of rice paper with it. Without the roof, the playhouse started to collapse.

Gordon screamed and hid his head in his laptop.

The walls of the playhouse skewed out of position and for a moment Gordon and I were sitting in a diamond-shaped playhouse with no roof. The sky looked very big and blue.

The lugs of plastic holding the walls together wrenched from their sockets and the house caved in on us.

'Arghhh!' Gordon crawled out of the wreckage and scrabbled to get a can out of his briefcase. He sprayed himself from head to toe with disinfectant. 'Don't ask me to get into an enclosed space with Freddo ever again,' he said.

'No need. The plan is set.' I waved my notebook in the air. 'Kepler 22b, here I come!'

10

The Truth About Cryogenics

Gordon said I had to be naked to be frozen alive.

I disagreed. I did not have the Kendal nudist DNA in my blood.

The mission team were crammed in the Kendal family bathroom to help me practise cryogenics.

'Clothing will act as an insulator,' Gordon said. 'Basic science.'

'Clothing is important to Keplerites like me,' I said.

'What's the problem?' Freddo said. 'Get naked!'

'No way!' I pulled up my hood and drew my fists into my sleeves.

'Are you serious about wanting to get back to Kepler 22b?' Freddo asked. 'Because I'm a bit concerned that you're not really taking this seriously.'

That's the sort of friend Freddo is. Totally sarcastic.

In the end, I wore:

'I don't think I need to practise cryogenics in advance of actually going,' I said, rubbing my hands over my arms but it didn't make the mega goose pimples go away. I hate being cold, but Dad won't have the heating on during the day. That's another reason why I must be an alien. The surface temperature of Kepler 22b is 22°C. Much warmer than my human home on Earth. I don't belong here so I was just going to have to put up with the inconvenience of being frozen alive.

'How much ice do we have?' Gordon said.

My contribution: three ice-cube trays with 18 cubes in each = 54 cubes

Freddo's contribution: eight mega bags of ice packed in his gran's shopping trolley. (Freddo's family always know how to get their hands on the right things at the right time. They always have Furbies in stock on their market stall right up until Christmas Eve.)

Gordon's contribution: a Thermos flask.

'The Cryopractitioner's Secret Ingredient,' Gordon said. 'Now is the time to tell us if you've changed your mind.' An evil scientist's grin spread across his face as he pulled on a pair of surgical gloves. He was loving this. Experimenting on a real live alien. Some kids like setting fire to things, others like blowing stuff up. For Gordon, freezing me solid was just as exciting.

For me, freezing me solid was just one step on the road to Kepler 22b.

'I haven't changed my mind,' I said. 'Get on with it.' My human family were downstairs watching the match. We had less than two hours before one of them would be hammering on the door to the bathroom.

'Then I shall proceed.' Gordon straightened his glasses and rolled up his sleeves. He shoved a thermometer under my tongue. It was lucky I didn't bite it, my chattering teeth were totally out of control. 'Thirty-seven degrees centigrade. Still normal.'

For a human, I thought.

'Shall I put in the ice now?' Freddo pulled out a huge bag of melting ice.

'Not yet,' Gordon said. 'We have to get his body temperature down in stages, otherwise the shock could kill him.'

Gordon spoke to Freddo, not me, which was very rude, but I couldn't say anything as I had a glass tube stuck under my tongue. If I opened my jaws, my teeth would snap on the glass and break the thermometer in two. If I swallowed glass fragments I wouldn't need to go into cryostasis – I'd die of internal bleeding here on Earth.

Mission failed.

Maybe it was a good thing the best friend telepathy wasn't working, because my brain was screaming at me not to do it.

Freddo and Gordon looked at me expectantly.

If I backed out now the mission would be over and

I would be stuck in my unhappy life on Earth forever. I looked at the chilly bathwater. Which was worse?

The moment had come.

I stepped into the bath.

Ice or no ice, it was flipping freezing. My feet turned instant ice blue and a rash of goose pimples charged up my body, making my few body hairs stand on end. I think it was my body's instinctive attempt at keeping me warm but it was failing. I reckoned my temperature must have dropped twenty degrees instantly.

Gordon the Geek peered at my thermometer.

'No change yet,' Gordon said. 'Time to submerge. We've got to get that temperature down otherwise your body will melt the ice, rather than ice freezing your internal organs solid.'

I'd never taken a bath in cold water before. I wrapped my tongue around the thermometer, clenched my lips together and sat, sinking my shivering body into the water.

I didn't know cold water could hurt. From the waist down, my poor Keplerite body was gripped in a chilly vice.

'Lie down! Lie down!' Gordon the Geek, my second best friend, put his hands on my shoulders and pushed me backwards. The icy water lapped over my chest, ending in a stranglehold around my neck. Only my head and bent knees were out of the water. My head because I was supposed to be freezing not drowning and my knees because I'm too tall to lie flat in the bath.

'Flipping freezing,' I said. But it sounded like 'Flnnnnrng freeezzzrng,' what with the thermometer and my chattering teeth.

'You've got a long way to go yet.' Gordon checked the thermometer. 'Still thirty-seven degrees.'

'No!' I shook my head vigorously, willing the red line to slip further down the tube. Surely my body temperature must have dropped enough by now.

'How long has he got to stay in there?' Freddo asked. He was playing with a piece of Mum's dental floss. He'd wrapped it around each tooth in turn so that it looked like white string braces. Not that he needed it with his great teeth and most snoggable mouth award.

'Ages,' Gordon said. 'There is no change in temperature yet.'

He had to be wrong. I had absolutely no feeling in my body. I was already well on the way to cryostasis.

'Maybe we should drain this water away and top

up with fresher, colder water from the tap?' Freddo said.

Gordon put his hand in the bath and ripped it out mega quick.

'No need. It's still cold.' Gordon peered at the thermometer again. 'Aha! It's down to thirty-six degrees at last. Freddo – the ice!' he said triumphantly.

I noticed he didn't ask me if I still wanted to be frozen alive. I didn't know the answer anyway. I didn't know much about anything any more. Even though my head wasn't under the water, my brain had already turned into a zombie's ice lolly.

My two best friends, Gordon the Geek and Freddo the Farting Freak stood over me and tipped ice into the bath.

I had ice between my toes. Ice crammed under my armpits. Ice piled up on my chest.

My knees stuck up above the sea of mini icebergs. Freddo thrust a bag stuffed with slushy ice over that last bit of visible skin and draped another unopened bag of ice over my head.

They didn't pile the ice on top of my underpants. I guess they realised the contents had already gone into hibernation.

Gordon held his Thermos flask in front of my

face. I nodded. He took off the lid. Smoke curled up from the opening. Whatever the 'Cryogenic Practitioner's Secret Ingredient' was, I was ready for it. Gordon poured something in the gap between my frozen feet at the bottom of the bath.

A cloud of billowing smoke erupted over the surface of the bath water. It spread out over my chest and head, engulfing me completely. The temperature of the freezing bath water dropped another zillion degrees, squeezing the last warm breath out of my body.

My jaw dropped open. The thermometer dangled from my iceberg lip. I breathed in the weird dry smoke that didn't smell of anything. The chill entered my lungs and spread through my body from the inside out.

Then a really weird thing happened. Instead

of feeling cold, I started feeling warm. It wasn't a warmth I'd ever felt before, but my teeth stopped chattering and the surface of my body glowed hot, as if I was wearing some sort of fiery onesie. Maybe being cryogenically frozen wasn't so bad after all.

My brain and my body weren't on the same planet any more. My brain was already in Kepler 22b. My body was somewhere else a million miles away. In the space in between, a geeky kid peered into my face. I knew him from somewhere. His glasses were familiar. A knobbly hand reached out and turned the weird tube sticking out of my mouth.

'Thirty-five degrees. It's working.' His mouth cracked open and I could see a row of teeth and a pink tongue.

'Show me,' another familiar voice said.

I was aware of someone with a mouth full of string.

I might have known him once.

A voice cackled. Another howled. Only there weren't two of them now. Two. Four. Eight. Sixty-four. The faces multiplied rapidly until all I could see was a million cackling morons.

Then, just like the portrait on the Wall of Wonders, the alien known as Daniel Kendal blacked out.

11

The Big Thaw

'Wake up! Wake up!' Something solid hit my face and my cheeks exploded with 10,000 volts of pain.

Something rough rubbed over my arms and legs, turning them into a couple of zinging electrified eels.

'Hand me those hot water bottles.' A fluffy warmth was pressed under my armpits.

'Wake up! Do you think we should call the ambulance?' These were the words I heard but I can't remember what order they came in. Blurry faces, loads of shouting and the excruciating pain of heat applied to my cryogenically frozen body.

These Keplerites were expert at defrosting their species *and* they spoke English. Somewhere in amongst the ice crystals, I remembered thinking, *I've arrived.*

'Thank you,' I said, even though I was in total agony.

'He's alive!' a voice shrieked. It sounded just like Mum. My human mum who had brought me up on Earth.

What was Mum doing on Kepler 22b? I thought I was the only alien around here.

I flickered my eyelids and checked out my home planet.

Doctor Who posters on the wall.

Battered Buzz Lightyear hanging from the ceiling.

Stick collection on the window sill.

That's when I realised I wasn't on Kepler 22b. I was in my bedroom. The one at 26 Beechwood Road on Earth.

I opened my eyes properly so I could be a hundred per cent certain I *was* still on Earth.

My human mum and dad stood by my bed. Mum with staring eyes. Dad's forehead lined with worry.

Hot blood thumped through my veins, defrosting my confusion.

I wasn't on Kepler 22b. Freddo, Gordon and I

were only trying out the freezing process, I hadn't made the journey yet. I was still on Earth. I hadn't gone anywhere.

'Daniel, look at me,' Mum said and slapped my face again.

'That's child abuse,' I said.

'Thank goodness. He's back from the dead.' She threw herself on me, smothering me with her hair. I didn't have the strength to throw her off but it was pretty tragic that I had survived the deep freeze only to be suffocated by my human mother.

'I'm calling Childline,' I said as I spat out a mouthful of hair.

'Childline? They can't help you. It's a psychiatrist you need,' Mum said.

'Calm down, Liz. Calm down,' Dad said. 'It was just a prank. Gordon and Fred said they were doing an experiment with liquid nitrogen for science club.'

'We need to speak to their teacher. They nearly killed him.'

'They were trying to work out how long a body can survive in freezing water,' Dad said, and even though I was still defrosting, I think he was laughing.

'Did they force you?' Mum patted my burning cheek.

'No,' I said.

'If you're being bullied at school, I need to know about it.'

'It was an experiment that went wrong.' My mind was clear now. Gordon and Freddo must have made up some story about science club.

'Don't they experiment on rats any more?' Mum said.

'The RSPCA wouldn't like it,' I murmured.

'You made yourself a giant guinea pig instead?'

'I think I need a sleep now,' I said. Mum's shrieks were giving my frozen brain a headache.

'Yes of course.' Mum patted my hand and I let out a guinea pig squeak. 'I'm going to go and look up hypothermia on the computer, in case you need to be in hospital.'

'Where are Gordon and Freddo?' I said.

'Gone home! They are banned from coming round ever again!' Mum stormed out, banging the open door against the wall. Dad followed her, still smirking.

Alone at last. The experiment had worked. I could survive being frozen and defrosted, but I didn't want to do it too often. Next time would be the real thing.

The day I shipped out to Kepler 22b.

We needed to move on to step two. How was I going to get to Kepler 22b?

12

The Boy Who Came From Earth

Because Mum thought I'd nearly died, she said I could have the week off school. She arranged to work from home for a week and even left Timmy at nursery so she could look after me.

But when she said I had to stay home for a week, she meant I had to stay in bed. Über-boring!

She gave me the bell from Jessie's bicycle and told me to ring it if I needed anything. She meant it, too.

Ring. Ring. Drink of water, please.

Ring. Ring. Could I have some biscuits?

Ring. Ring. Any chance of an extra pillow?

By lunchtime she took the bell downstairs, muttering about slavery.

5 Alien Activities to do
When Imprisoned in a Human Bed

1. Re-read every issue of *The Beano*.
2. Re-organise Deadly Venomous Snakes cards.
3. Count the cracks in the ceiling.
4. Have a little sleep.
5. I can't think of another one.

By mid-afternoon, I was ready to get up and start researching which countries had the technology to get me to Kepler 22b.

'Can I come down and use the computer?' I asked Mum when she came up with a snack.

'No. I need to do some work.'

'Can I watch TV?'

'No. I can't concentrate if the TV is on.'

My human mum is very fond of the word 'no'.

'Why do we have the computer in the same room as the TV?' I said.

'Not again!' Mum sighed. 'The computer lives in the sitting room because I like to know what you're doing on the computer.'

'Why?'

Mum left the room without answering.

Human parents don't understand the basic needs of alien kids like me.

I bet kids on Kepler 22b have their own computers or some other alien technology. And they are going to share it with me. The Boy Who Came From Earth. They'll probably think I'm exotic. They might even think I'm cool.

<u>My Personal Belongings on Kepler 22b</u>

1. A laptop wired into my brain. So I'd know everything all of the time without having to ask anyone.

2. A teleporter so I could go anywhere instantly without having to walk.

3. A full set of fifty Deadly Venomous Alien cards so I knew who I could be friends with.

4. A telepathic phone so all I had to do was think 'Freddo' and I'd be able to talk to him without opening my mouth.

5. A loft bed. I've always wanted one of those but Mum keeps saying no.

I had to switch off my alien fantasy pretty quickly as Jessie came in and plonked herself on the end of my Earth bed.

'You still here, Oddbod?' she said.

'Yes, but I'm not odd. I'm an alien, remember?'

Her face looked puzzled for a moment but then her lip-glossed mouth cracked into a smile. 'You really need to meet Serena Blake.'

'Who is Serena Blake?'

'My year. Dyed black hair cut in a bob. She reckons she was taken into a spaceship by one of your lot, then dumped back on Earth when they'd finished with her.'

'She's human though, isn't she?'

'Yeah, but she's in love with little green men. Martians. The Man in the Moon. Whatever. She goes on about them the whole time. She's nuts.' Jessie

stood up. 'Mum says she's finished on the computer. But you can't go on it because I am.' She poked her human tongue out and left – slamming the door, of course.

Jessie is THE worst sort of human sister. The sooner I leave this planet the better and that wasn't going to happen if I was chained to the bed. I needed my team and the Geek's technology to get me out of here.

'You need to stay home all week,' Mum said when I went downstairs.

'But I'm not ill.'

She held me by both hands and looked into my eyes.

'You nearly died,' she said.

'If I was so near death, how come you didn't take me to hospital?'

'I decided it was best to care for you at home,' Mum said.

'It had nothing to do with not wanting to miss the penalty shootout?'

Mum blushed.

Cryostasis messes with your brain, but once you've thawed out, the brain works perfectly. Mum and Dad thought I was still in the fuzzy phase of hypothermia when they had a row about whether I should go to hospital.

But I'd heard every word. And understood them too.

Dad had said, 'He's sleeping now, we shouldn't disturb him.'

Mum had said, 'But I'm worried.'

Dad had said, 'If his lips are still blue when the match is over, we'll take him.'

I happen to know that match went to extra time and penalties. By the time it was over I had fully thawed out and hadn't died in the process.

No one took me to hospital.

I picked up Jessie's bicycle bell from the kitchen table and rang it endlessly.

Mum snatched the bell out of my hand and threw it in the bin. 'You can go back to school tomorrow.'

13

Spitting Teachers and Other Problems

The desks in my classroom are grouped in pairs. Five pairs of desks in three columns. I sit next to Freddo, of course, because he's my best friend and no one else wants to sit next to a long-legged alien like me or a crisp-encrusted fart monster. But things had changed while I'd been in the deep freeze.

Gordon was sitting in my seat next to Freddo. Gordon's usual seat was empty.

'What's going on?' I said.

'Wasn't sure you'd want to be mates any more since I nearly killed you,' Freddo said and kept his eyes focused on the inside of his crisp packet.

'You didn't nearly kill me. It was voluntary cryostasis.'

'That's not what your mum said. She went on and on about me bullying you into it. She told school we're not allowed to sit next to each other in case I try to kill you again.' He bent down and tied his shoelaces. He didn't seem to realise he was wearing trainers with Velcro.

Thanks to Mum, I had to sit centre aisle, front row, right next to a girl.

'Welcome back!' Mr Pitdown shouted in a totally fake way. I could tell by the evil glint in his eye he wished I'd stayed at home.

At that moment I wished I was still at home too. I didn't want to sit at the desk nearest to him and his ski jump moustache.

His spit stank of garlic. Aliens are like vampires. Totally allergic to garlic. I don't know how Gordon has coped with sitting in the front row all year. No wonder he sprays his whole desk with disinfectant at the start and end of every lesson.

'I'm pleased you've found your new seat, where I can keep an eye on you. Make sure you're okay,' Mr Pitdown shouted so everyone could hear.

A snigger rippled through the class.

Oh great! I'd been promoted from class misfit to class wimp. I thumped down in my new seat and glared at Mr Pitdown. I'd been off school for one day and I'd already lost my best friend as well as the only hint of class kudos I'd ever had.

'Hi,' the girl next to me said. She was the one with the handlebar pigtails. Her name's Susan but I'd never spoken to her before. She pulled her hair round the edge of her jaw and popped the end into her mouth.

'Sorry you were ill,' Susan said. 'Are you better now?'

'Hmph!' I made that noise because I didn't want to break my personal record for not having spoken to a girl ever (except my sister who doesn't count).

Sitting in the front row of the class is a total

nightmare if you want to make plans to escape from this solar system. Mr Pitdown is a walker. The sort of teacher who strides backwards and forwards as he talks. I guess he does it because he doesn't have enough time to go to the gym because of all the marking he has to do.

I've heard other teachers moaning about the same thing. Don't they realise if they set us easier work, we wouldn't make so many mistakes and they'd only have to put a tick at the end and the marking wouldn't take so long?

This is my analysis of how teachers waste their time marking:

30 ticks TAKES LESS TIME TO WRITE THAN 30 x 19 spelling mistakes PLUS 30 x 67 punctuation errors PLUS 30 comments about not having written enough.

Teachers can be totally thick sometimes.

Anyway, Mr Pitdown does his workout right there in the class. Today he even worked up a sweat as, every time he crossed the room, he had to jump over my legs. It dripped down to join the spittle on the edge of his moustache.

Remind me to bring an umbrella tomorrow.

He walked backwards and forwards and jumped over my legs so much, I couldn't concentrate on how I was going to get to Kepler 22b.

At the end of the lesson Mr Pitdown made me swap back with Gordon. He must have decided that it wasn't such a great idea having a long-legged alien in the front row.

Result! I could get back to making my plans for getting out of here. But three brains are better than one. I decided to call another mission meeting.

Вы говорите по-русски?

Freddo, Gordon and I hung out in the dark corner under the science block fire-escape to discuss what to do next.

'We've worked out the cryostasis – sort of – but how am I actually going to get my frozen body up there?' I waved my hand in the direction of outer space.

Freddo stuffed a fistful of crisps in his mouth and started munching.

Gordon was wearing his laptop as usual. His hands were on the keyboard and it was impossible to tell if he was listening to me as his fingers danced across the keys.

Once again the best friend telepathy radar must

have been faulty. My first and second best friends were not picking up my thoughts. They weren't listening even when I went to the effort of speaking, so I had to shout.

'Hello? Is anyone listening to me?'

'Sure we're listening, but you're not saying much,' Freddo said. He ripped open his empty crisp packet and licked every drop of grease from the inside.

'I'm looking for suggestions,' I said.

'Join NASA, I guess,' Freddo said.

'No point,' Gordon said. 'The space shuttle is over and the USA has no manned space programme in the pipeline any more. You'll have to go to Russia.'

'Russia?'

'Only way to get to space is via Russia.' Gordon pushed his glasses up the bridge of his nose. 'Unless China has a space programme they're not telling us about and if it's that secret, they're not going to let *you* join, are they?'

Remind me to borrow a Russian language course from the library.

'How do I get to Russia?' I asked.

'The next flight to Moscow takes off at three-thirty,' Gordon read from his computer screen. 'But

I'm not sure that leaves you enough time to get through security. It's one o'clock now.'

'Do you think if I show up at the Russian space agency offering to go to Kepler 22b under cryostasis, they'll let me?'

'No!' Freddo said and flicked his balled crisp packet at me.

'Why not?' Gordon said. 'They're not allowed to use animals any more.'

'Okay. But I can't go today. Or this week even. It's the series finale of *Doctor Who* on Saturday and I'm not missing it. Anyway, how much is the airfare?'

Gordon briefly turned his computer round and showed me a spreadsheet.

FLIGHT CLASS	PRICE
Business	£1,400
Economy	£670
Budget	£150

'How much have you got?' I pulled out 27p from my pocket and held it out to my friends.

Freddo had £1.86 but he needed £1.50 for chips on his way home so he only gave me 36p.

'Gordon?'

Gordon didn't flinch. He kept on tapping.

Have I told you that Gordon is tight? He's my mate and everything but he never has any money. He doesn't eat lunch, he doesn't eat crisps and I've never seen him drink anything but water.

Freddo and I have this theory that Gordon is saving up for something. He must get pocket money and he does a bit of PC support for older people who don't know how to use Facebook. So what does he spend his money on?

'Gordon, can you lend me the money to fly to Russia?'

'No,' he said.

'I'll pay you back.'

'No.'

I could tell that he was only pretending to look at his laptop. Actually he was ignoring me.

If Gordon was an alien he would be able to read my thoughts and would know how important it is for me to get to Kepler 22b. But Gordon is not an alien, he's human, and he was not going to lend me the money because he's so tight. Grandad would say, 'Tight as a frog's backside – and that's watertight.' Gordon was an über-tight frog with the associated backside.

I didn't need to create a spreadsheet to tell me I didn't have enough money to get to Russia.

It didn't matter because there was probably no way of sending money back from Kepler 22b. I'm not even sure what currency they use.

'So how am I going to earn the money for the flight to Russia?' I said.

There was an ominous silence.

Have you noticed there are very limited opportunities for kids to make money? I could do jobs at home, but Mum and Dad only pay twenty pence a time so it was going to take me aeons to earn enough to go to Russia and by that time I'd be an adult and would have missed out on my teenage years on Kepler 22b.

'Halloween next week,' Freddo said. 'We could go trick or treating.'

'What use is a bag of jellied skulls and a mini Mars bar?' I said.

'We could get some awesome costumes,' Freddo said, ignoring me.

'Jessie's got a witch's outfit, you can borrow it if you like,' I said.

'Sweet shop,' Gordon said.

There was a weird silence as Freddo and I tried

to work out how to go trick or treating dressed as a sweet shop.

'If we get enough trick or treat booty we could open a sweet shop at break times and sell the sweets to the other kids,' Gordon explained.

Have I ever referred to Gordon as The Geek? I meant to call him *Gordon the Genius*.

15

The Great Halloween Transformation

First we had to get some awesome Halloween costumes. The better the costumes, the better the booty. No one was going to give us any sweets if we had some lame sheet with holes for eyes. The good thing about having an older sister is she has loads of make-up and hair gunk. I reckoned I could save money on a mask and go for face painting and a crazy hairstyle.

Or I could wrap myself in toilet paper and become an Egyptian mummy. But what if it rained? I didn't want to be flushed away. I needed to choose something safer.

I couldn't make up my mind whether to dress up as Dracula or a werewolf.

Vampires	Werewolves
Cool	Scary
Slicked back hair (loads of gel required)	Scruffy fur (already have scruffy hair, no gel required)
Only go out at night (okay because trick or treating happens at night)	Can't go out on the full moon (need to check the moon on Halloween)
Might be mistaken for a dead person and buried alive	Might be mistaken for a rabid dog and shot by the police

I had some plastic teeth from a party bag. I figured they'd work well for either a vampire or a werewolf, but I didn't know what to wear.

'What do werewolves wear?' I asked at breakfast.

Mum and Dad both picked up their mugs of tea with their right hands and took a sip at exactly the same time. The way they are in total harmony with each other freaks me out. They didn't answer.

'Werewolves don't exist,' Jessie said.

'They do in movies,' I said.

'Movies aren't real,' she said.

'Let me ask the question in another way. If I were to dress up as a werewolf on Halloween, what should I wear?'

'Nothing. Werewolves lose their clothes when they transform and they run around in their hairy naked bodies biting people.' Jessie grinned. 'Let me know when you're ready so I can take a photo and put it on Facebook. I've got one thousand, two hundred and thirty-five followers.'

I'm getting really worried that Jessie is thinking of becoming a nudist just like Mum and Dad used to be. Double urgh. Yuk. Gross. Teenage girls should keep their clothes on.

Mum woke up and started speaking. 'You could get some furry mittens and stick a bit of fur at the opening of your shirt. Seeing as you don't have any chest hair yet.'

Why are my family obsessed with bodies? Mine

and theirs? They are totally unsympathetic to my sensitive alien psyche. Aliens need to be dressed all the time.

I decided to go as Count Dracula. Count Dracula had really bad clothes sense but he never went around naked.

I sneaked into Jessie's room to rifle through her make-up. She didn't have white face paint. She only had something called Instant Copper Bronze but I think they put the wrong label on the tube because when I squeezed some out onto my fingertips it was white. Result – I slapped it on really thickly. She had some red lipstick and the way I put it on made it look like I'd just gouged my mouth around someone's jugular vein. I also managed to stab myself in the eye with an eyeliner pencil and the bloodshot look added to the overall impression.

Count Dracula was ready.

16

Trick or Treat?

Freddo and Gordon met me on the corner as they were still banned from my house. I was totally unimpressed with their costumes.

'What's this?' I tugged at the sheet covering Gordon's head. He hadn't even bothered to cut the eyeholes out.

The sheet twitched as if the geek inside was shrugging. I could hear the tap of fingers on keys so there was no point having an argument with him.

'Where's your costume?' I asked Freddo. He wore jeans and a hoody as usual. I couldn't see his face in the dark. He turned suddenly and his eyeballs popped out and leapt towards me.

'Arghhh!' I screamed like someone out of a horror movie. Only I wasn't acting.

'Ha! Fooled you,' Freddo said.

'How d'you do it?' I said when my heart rate had slowed down enough for me to speak.

Freddo showed me the trick. He had a black mask and had treated some pop-out eyeball glasses with glow-in-the-dark paint. He just had to shine his torch in his face for twenty seconds, then his eyeballs glowed for another twenty. He looked pretty freakish.

Other Trick or Treaters Out That Night

37 witches
A trio dressed as The Lion, The Witch and The Wardrobe
5 vikings
124 vampires/Draculas with better costumes than mine
2 Wonder Women and 3 Supergirls – all adults
2 Batmen – father and son
1 Frankenstein's monster
89 ghosts (excluding Gordon) all wearing sheets with holes for eyes
16 zombies
1 Justin Bieber lookalike followed by 9 screaming girls
6 pirates but only one had a parrot
2 police officers – though they might have been real

Most people wandering the streets should have already been in bed. The kids were so little they had to bring their mums and dads with them and the little monsters kept mistaking us for adults.

'Twick or tweat?' A little girl with a pink tutu and a witch's hat asked Freddo. She already had a plastic cauldron stuffed with sweets and chocolates. We had nothing so Freddo decided to go with the trick option.

He secretly shone the torch in his face and then lurched at the ballerina witch so that his glow-in-the-dark eyes flew out from his hood and knocked her hat off her head.

She dropped her cauldron and bawled her head off.

'What do you think you're doing? Scaring a little girl like that?' A woman with green skin and purple string hair came running over waving her broomstick at us. 'Go away, you horrid boys. You're spoiling it for the little ones.'

'*Trick* or *treat* – yeah?' Freddo said, but the witch mother was too busy stuffing a chocolate spider into the baby witch's mouth.

The first house in the street was decorated with pumpkins and glittery bats at the window. We rang the bell.

An old lady wearing laddered pink tights, a silver mini-dress and a tiara answered. She waved a silver wand topped with a glittering star.

'Entertain me,' she said. 'Come on, earn your treat.' She waved the wand at us again. 'Sing! Dance! I used to be a showgirl, you know,' she said and she twirled round.

She expected us to perform to earn our sweets! This hadn't been part of the mission plan.

She spun around again, urging us to join in but I wish she hadn't bothered. Her silver dress had split at the back, revealing a roll of wrinkled flesh and the top of her underwear. It was enough to turn Count Dracula vegetarian.

Luckily the ghost with no eyes was blind. Gordon's voice piped up from under his sheet. '*We wish you a merry Christmas. We wish you a merry Christmas.*'

Freddo and I joined in with a gruff, '*And a happy new year.*'

'Hopeless. The wrong season and everything. I suggest you rehearse "Bat Out of Hell" for next year,' the old lady said. 'Now let me inspect your costumes.'

She tapped each of us in turn with her wand and like idiots we stomped round in a circle. I never knew Halloween could be so humiliating but we had to raise the money for the flight to Russia somehow.

'Nice mask but no effort anywhere else,' she said to Freddo and handed him one boiled sweet.

'What are you supposed to be?' she said to me.

'Count Dracula.'

'I didn't know vampires were so tall. You must have a massive coffin. Anyway, isn't he supposed to have a white face not a brown streaky one? I thought you were a werewolf. Two sweets for trying.' The sweets were sticky, as if they had been in the packet for five or six years.

She turned to Gordon. 'Are you sure there's a real person under that sheet? It's not just a teddy bear or something? How can he see where he's going?'

'He's blind,' I said which wasn't a total lie. If Gordon takes off his glasses he can't see a thing. 'We're looking after him.'

'Poor thing. Here, take the rest of the packet.'

The sell-by date on the sweet packet was sometime in the last millennium. There was no way we could sell them.

'What did she mean, "brown streaky face"?' I said when we were safely back on the pavement.

'You've got a brown streaky face.' Freddo nodded and his eyes flopped towards me, bouncing up and down on their springs.

I ducked down and looked at myself in a car wing mirror. Sure enough, Count Dracula looked like he'd been under a sun lamp for hours.

'I can't understand it. The stuff was white when it came out of the tube.'

'What was it called on the outside?' Gordon asked.

'Instant copper bronze or something,' I said.

'Fake tan,' Freddo said. 'Goes on white, skin goes brown later. You can always borrow Gordon's sheet for school tomorrow if it doesn't come off.'

'What do you mean? I don't want to be a vampire with a streaky werewolf face forever. I'm an alien.'

'They won't mind on Kepler 22b,' the ghost with no eyes said. 'They'll think it's an Earth thing.'

He was right. The rest of my species on Kepler 22b would be so pleased to see me, they wouldn't mind what I looked like. My class at school would not be so sympathetic.

'Dad's got something called Miracle Stain Removing Cream,' Freddo said. 'It's supposed to be for cleaning ovens but I'm sure it'll do the trick.'

If Freddo really thought I was going to plaster my face with skin-eating cream, he was wrong. I was stuck with a brown streaky face forever.

'Let's get a move on,' I said. The sooner I was on

my way to Kepler 22b the better.

My face can't have been too bad as the next few houses didn't make any comment about our costumes, they just gave us a few sweets.

'One point six seven.' Gordon's voice was more muffled than usual because of the sheet. 'That's how many sweets we're averaging. One point six seven per house in the street. It's going to take us a long time to get enough for the sweet shop.'

He was right. My carrier bag contained two rubber snakes (small ones), six cola bottles and three oranges. Oranges! Who gave oranges at Halloween?

'We can't give up yet. How much do you think we can sell this lot for?'

'Twenty-five pence. Thirty pence on a good day,' the muffled voice answered.

No way was that enough to get me to Russia.

The lights were off at the next house and there was no carved pumpkin on the step.

Freddo rang the bell anyway as we were desperate.

'Trick or treat,' he said in an upbeat voice when the door opened. The man did not need to dress up in a costume. His own white hair and matching bushy eyebrows made him look like some nut-job professor.

'Wait here,' he said.

The man returned with a huge bucket. Things were looking up.

'Trick!' he shouted and chucked a bucket full of water over us. 'That'll teach you. Scroungers!' He slammed the door in our faces.

'That's it. I'm going home.' Gordon pulled a sopping sheet from his head and threw it on the floor. 'I'm not helping you any more.' He tipped his laptop and water trickled onto the pavement.

'It'll dry out,' I said.

Gordon the Geek, my second best friend, turned his back on me and walked away.

17

A Spark of Genius

Okay, I admit it, the trick or treating thing was a waste of time. The grand total of our fund-raising efforts was two jelly snakes. Freddo ate the cola bottles. The oranges went mouldy. The fake tan turned out to be temporary so I was spared the humiliation of being called Mr Pumpkinhead at school.

Luckily Gordon's laptop did dry out, otherwise I'd have lost my second best friend and I'd have been stuck on Earth forever.

5 November is Bonfire Night. I didn't fancy the firework show. Looking up at the night sky knowing my real home and family were 'out there' would just depress me. I managed to persuade Mum

it was better for me to stay inside because of the hypothermia and amazingly she unbanned Freddo and Gordon so they could keep me company.

'Aren't you supposed to be exercising?' Freddo said as he stared out of the window. 'You know, getting fit to be an astronaut?'

'What's the point?' I said. 'No money. No Russian space programme. No Kepler 22b.'

'Have you ever seen *ET*?' Gordon asked.

We were in my room. Freddo wanted to see the fireworks so we switched off all the lights, opened the curtains and my two best friends lazed on the floor watching the pyrotechnics while I lay on my bed looking at the ceiling and thinking how far away Kepler 22b seemed now.

'*ET*? Have you seen it?' Gordon's voice came out of the darkness. His laptop was closed. Freddo said the light spoilt the firework show. There was a streetlight right outside my window so it wasn't pitch black but I didn't put him straight. Gordon needed to wean himself off that computer or he'd turn into an addict.

'*ET* is for kids,' I said, just to humour him.

'Yeah, but did you see it when you were a kid?'

'Sure.'

Bang!

'That's a good one.' Freddo pointed out of the window as more and more rockets exploded overhead.

'ET was abandoned on Earth,' Gordon said. 'He was an alien kid like you.'

'He wasn't like me. He could hardly speak and he was bald and he was very short even though he had a long neck. Tell him, Freddo, I am not ET.'

'Whooo!' Freddo said to the fireworks outside.

'ET didn't have to go to Russia to join the space programme,' Gordon said. 'He called up his mum and dad to come and get him.'

There was a fat, black pause in the room. You could almost see it, only the lights were out.

'Are you suggesting we try to phone Kepler 22b?' I sat up in bed. Maybe it was time to promote Gordon the Geek to first best friend.

'They might not realise they left you behind, or maybe they think you're happy with your human family after all this time.'

'Maybe you're not an alien after all.' Freddo pushed his face up against the window, smearing the glass with snot. He licked his finger and added spit to the slime. 'This is an alien.' He pointed to something which could have been a picture on the glass. It had two heads.

'Shut up, Freddo! Gordon, I've said it before and I'll say it again, YOU ARE A GENIUS. How do I phone home?'

The Supreme Communication Device

Freddo and Gordon drive me mad sometimes but they are the best mates an oddbod alien misfit like me could ever have hoped for.

It took him a week but this time Gordon had truly excelled himself.

'Behold! The Supreme Communication Device!' Gordon said as he opened his briefcase.

'What's that?' Freddo reached out and stabbed a greasy crisp-flavoured finger at a USB port stuck in the middle.

Gordon snatched the circuit board away. 'I've constructed this in a static-free environment.'

Freddo licked his finger. 'You're all right, Gordon. It was cheese and onion flavour today. They were out of static.'

Gordon moved his device out of Freddo's reach.

'I am missing two vital components. A keyboard and a communications satellite.'

'We could use your laptop,' I said. 'That has a keyboard.'

'No we could not,' Gordon said.

And that's when I realised Gordon was my SECOND best friend for a reason. He wasn't prepared to cannibalise his laptop for the mission.

'Okay, so where can we get a keyboard?' I said.

'Leave that to me,' Freddo said.

Freddo was the best mate an alien could have. He always delivered. No doubt his dad has a garage full of laptops.

With Freddo supplying the keyboard and Gordon building the communication device, it was only fair I supplied the satellite. There was one on the front of the house. It was connected to the TV downstairs.

'When you say "satellite", what exactly do you mean?' I asked Gordon the Geek.

Gordon took off his glasses and cleaned them on the end of his tie.

Whenever he takes his glasses off I'm shocked at how small his eyes are without them. I guess he has a small head. I reckon Gordon is small because he saves his lunch money rather than buying lunch with it. He'll never grow as tall as me if he doesn't eat. And then I remembered he won't grow as tall as me because he's human.

'Any sort of satellite dish should work.' Gordon put his glasses back on. 'I'll have to reverse the polarity to make it transmit rather than receive. It should be able to relay back to the central satellite and then to any other communication devices up there.'

He pointed at the ceiling light, although I think he meant the satellites up in space. 'So long as someone from Kepler 22b is monitoring our communications, they should hear us.'

'Someone?' Freddo said. 'Don't you mean some*thing*? I wonder if Keplerites have loads of tentacles and acid for blood.'

'You've been watching too many movies and are now getting fiction muddled up with the facts.' I glared at Freddo. Just when things were getting serious, Freddo had to get all silly again. 'I am *an* alien, who looks like this.' I pointed to my chest. 'Not *the* Alien who is in a movie you are too young to watch anyway.' Freddo was always watching films with his big brother that were totally *not* age appropriate.

'Are you sure?' Freddo grinned. 'Shall I check out the airing cupboard to see if you're incubating eggs or something?'

There are times when I want to grind Freddo's face into the carpet.

So how come he's my best friend?

We started at play group on the same day. I sat on the carpet listening to a story with the other kids while Freddo ran round and round the outside of the circle pushing a toy vacuum cleaner and shouting, 'To finity and behind.' I thought he was pretty cool.

The next day, I joined in the vacuuming and we never listened to story time again. We've been best friends ever since.

Freddo wasn't really interested in helping me. He said he could provide a keyboard, but Gordon needed a satellite too. I bet Freddo's dad had a garage full of them, but for some reason he didn't want me to have one. I was a hundred per cent committed to this mission even if he wasn't. I was prepared to do anything if it meant going to Kepler 22b, even upsetting my human family.

'I've got a satellite,' I told Gordon.

The Problem With Satellites

I knew my human family would be cheesed off when they found out I had removed their only way to watch TV, but I reckoned they'd forgive me when they realised I'd swiped the satellite to further my mission to relocate myself to Kepler 22b. I'm not really one of the family, after all.

Reasons My Family Will Be Pleased I've Left Earth

1. Timmy can have my room. It's much bigger than his bedroom and he'll be able to lay out all my old wooden railway and build a Lego city around

it using every single brick, just like I used to do. He'll love it.

2. Jessie has always said she wished I'd never existed so she'll be thrilled that I'm out of her life.

3. Mum will no longer have to carry huge 48-biscuit packs of Weetabix from the supermarket and she'll have more space on the top shelf for rice/pasta/beans. She won't be able to reach them, but she could always buy a step ladder that doesn't answer back.

4. Dad will be pleased that he'd no longer get a crick in his neck from looking up at me when he tells me off. He'll never have to visit the chiropractor again.

I reckoned my family would think that one measly satellite dish was a fair price to pay to be rid of me. But I hadn't left Earth yet and there might be a delay before my alien family came for me. I was a little nervous about what my human family would do to me during that time.

The next problem was that Mum and Dad were due back from work and Jessie would be home very soon. We only had three minutes to kidnap the satellite dish without being caught.

The other problem with kidnapping the Kendal family satellite dish is that it was attached to a vertical brick wall, and quite high up on the front of the house. Luckily, Freddo's dad had brilliant window-cleaner ladders.

Do you know how high a two-storey building is? About ten metres. That's high.

Freddo's dad's long, narrow ladder looked pretty flimsy propped up against the front wall of our house.

'That's high,' I said, looking up at the satellite dish.

'That's high,' Freddo said.

Fully extended, the ladder reached the skinny bit of wall between the satellite dish and my parents' bedroom window. To unscrew it, I needed to climb to the very top of the ladder and duck behind the dish to reach the screws.

Our house is semi-detached, which means that one side of our house is attached to next door. On the other side (the satellite side), our house is not attached to anything. There's a dark alley, a fence and another dark alley, then the wall of Mrs Fagan's house next door. That dark chasm of doom between the houses made the ladder look even narrower.

I would have been quite happy to stand around saying, 'That's high' all day if it meant I didn't have to climb that ladder.

'Up you go, then,' Freddo said.

'I thought you were here to help me,' I said.

'I supplied the ladder,' Freddo said.

'I'm supplying the satellite dish,' I said.

'Not unless you get it off the wall,' Freddo said.

He was right, of course. Without that satellite dish, I'd remain exiled on Earth forever.

I had no choice.

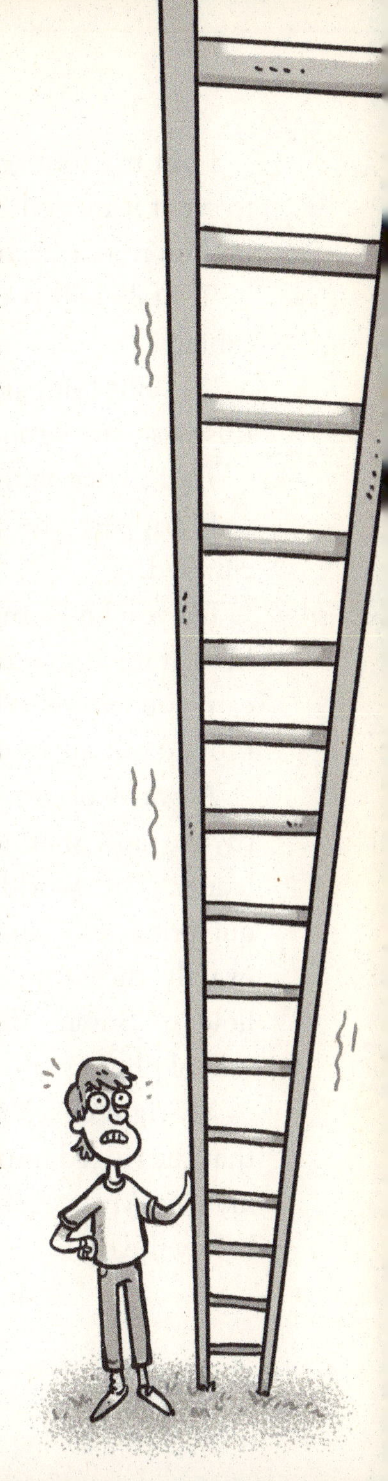

I put my foot on the bottom rung of the ladder to see if it moved. It was rock solid.

'You're not frightened, are you?' Freddo asked.

'If I fall, will you catch me?' I said, changing the subject.

'No. But I'll make sure your ashes are shipped to Russia so an astronaut can scatter them in space.'

That's what you call a best friend.

I gripped the ladder with both hands and climbed.

Do you know the meaning of the word 'vertigo'? Look it up in the dictionary. It's a good one and will earn you extra marks in an English test if you use it. I found out all about it on that ladder.

A wave of fear reared up from my Keplerite psyche and slammed my alien body against the ladder. The world was all wobbly and I was a quivering jellyfish in the middle of it all. It was exactly the same feeling that had made me grab hold of Susan Albright's hair at the top of the school photo scaffolding.

My right cheek pressed so hard against the rungs that the ridged imprint of the tread was tattooed to my face. My eyes stared unblinking at the pavement below me.

The ladder and I were super-glued together. The dark chasm of doom loomed large between my house and next door. Any minute it was going to leap up and swallow me whole.

'You all right, Dan?' Freddo called up to me.

I couldn't answer. Even my tongue was paralysed. I gripped the sides of the ladder and willed it to crash to the ground just to get it over with.

'Dan?' Freddo's voice seemed small down there on the pavement. I pressed my cheek further into the ladder and closed my eyes.

'Dan!' Freddo's voice was right by my ear now. 'Let go.' A greasy, crisp-flavoured hand yanked my fingers away from the ladder.

I couldn't open my eyes. I didn't want to see my best friend hanging precariously from the ladder over the chasm of doom. The same ladder that my poor, terrified, Keplerite body was stuck to.

'I've got you,' Freddo said. 'One step down.'

He nudged my left foot and somehow I plucked up the courage to move it down one rung.

'Now the other,' he said.

My other foot came down.

'Okay, two more steps.'

I managed to move each foot twice more and

then miraculously I was standing on the ground.

'It's high up there,' I said, my legs like two rubber bands.

'How would *you* know? You only made it to the fourth step.'

The downstairs window opened next door.

'Are you doing windows now, Daniel?' Mrs Fagan called. 'I'll give you five pounds if you clean mine front and back.'

Five pounds. It was more money than we'd made from our Halloween money-making scheme but I reckoned that I'd have to get further than the fourth rung of the ladder to do a really good job. So I turned her down and tried not to think too much about the crisp blue fiver that could have been mine.

'Catch me if I fall,' Freddo said. With a grin he sprinted up the ladder like a squirrel up a tree. Two minutes later he was back on the pavement with the satellite dish.

Freddo was the best friend ever. I was never going to complain about him again.

20

Hiding the Evidence

When something is at the top of a tall building, it seems quite small. When it's down on the ground, right next to you on the pavement, it's much bigger.

The satellite dish was HUGE.

I wasn't sure how Freddo had managed to de-install my family's satellite TV and get the dish down the ladder so quickly. Maybe his dad had been in the satellite business before he became a market trader.

'You stash this.' Freddo leant the huge dish against the wall. 'I'll go get the keyboard.' And he was gone.

I didn't hang around because:

a) if the police drove past they'd probably arrest me and that would be the end of my return to Kepler

22b. I reckoned if those Keplerites knew I had a criminal record, they wouldn't come and get me.

b) if Mum came home, the mission would be over for a completely different reason. She'd kill me for removing the dish. And once she'd finished killing me, she'd hand me over to Dad for more of the same. When I'd been well and truly murdered by my human parents, Jessie would take over. Alienicide x 3. Bad news! It was essential my family didn't find out who had stolen the satellite dish.

I needed to find the perfect hiding place.

Luckily there was a dark chasm of doom handy. I hid the dish in the alley between Mrs Fagan's house and ours.

That left the ladder.

When Freddo had brought the ladder round it had been a lot shorter. Somehow it had been collapsed down and stacked in a more manageable length. Fully extended, a ten-metre ladder is a tricky customer. I didn't know how to un-extend it and I was running out of time. Mum was due back from work any minute.

I reckoned the chasm of doom was big enough to swallow it whole, so I grabbed the ladder away from the house, meaning to floor it in one.

But the ladder had other ideas. First it tottered left, next it swung round to the right. Ten metres of untamed ladder reared above me like a giant cobra. Its head bobbed here and there, looking for a place to strike.

Then it found the perfect target. Mrs Fagan's brand new car. The ladder twirled round on one leg and it went into free-fall. I shut my eyes and waited for the crash.

Silence.

I opened my eyes, thinking maybe the cobra had decided to take me out instead and I was now unconscious or something.

But no. My hands still had hold of the ladder. It was stuck at a forty-five-degree angle.

The head of the ladder had entwined itself in a random wire suspended between our house and a telegraph pole further down the street.

The snake was tamed.

I eyed up the angle between the ladder and the ground, gave it a yank and at last the ladder crashed down in the chasm of doom. Right where I needed it.

Result!

I had no idea why there had been a wire leading to the corner of our house, but it wasn't there now.

It was still connected to the telegraph pole but the other end lay dead on the pavement. It wasn't spitting sparks or anything so it can't have been important.

What is a telegraph pole, anyway? I thought. Something to do with Morse code and telegrams. My human family were more sophisticated than that. They used the telephone and email to keep in touch. I reckoned Dad would be delighted to be rid of that random wire.

More importantly, the mission now owned a satellite dish. With Freddo's keyboard and Gordon's communication device, I was about to be reunited with my real family on Kepler 22b. I couldn't wait.

I'd only just got back into the house when Jessie came home from school.

'Speak to the hand, Oddbod,' she said, thrusting

her palm in my face. 'I'm getting together with my mates in a mega virtual hangout. We're going to annihilate Serena Blake!'

She rushed into the sitting room and switched on the computer. Then she poked her head around the door and said, 'Do not disturb. Yeah?'

Jessie slammed the door to the sitting room. I went up to my room to wait for Freddo and Gordon.

Every evening it's the same old 'Do Not Disturb' routine. I've never disturbed her boring virtual hangout and I wasn't going to start today, I had much more important communications to tackle before bedtime.

'Arghh!' Jessie screamed so loudly I could hear it through my tightly closed bedroom door. I wondered if maybe Serena Blake was annihilating her back, but I figured it wasn't any of my business.

My door flew open and Jessie came into my room.

'Have you been messing with the computer?' she said.

'No,' I said.

'There's no internet,' she said.

'Nothing to do with me,' I said.

'Arghhh!' she screamed.

Somehow, through all the racket, I heard the key in the front door.

'Mum's home,' I said.

'You are the most annoying brother and I wish you'd never been born,' Jessie yelled for no reason before she slammed the door and charged downstairs.

'I wasn't born. I was dumped, remember,' I shouted after her, but she didn't answer.

I suppose I was born on Kepler 22b. Or maybe on the journey to Earth.

There's an awful lot about life in the Kepler 22b world that I know nothing about.

But I know an awful lot about life on Earth. And Jessie the Random Mood queen is one thing I won't miss when I'm back with my alien family.

21

The Weird Case of the Hypnotic Laptop

I don't know why humans have to be so loud. My alien ears are very sensitive.

I plugged in my headphones and buried my head under my pillow. I think I might have suffocated if Freddo hadn't pulled the pillow off my face. Gordon was already in the corner tapping away on his laptop.

'Your sister's going mental downstairs,' Freddo said.

'She's already mental. Have you got the keyboard?'

Freddo plonked a cardboard box on my bed.

It wasn't any old box, it was the original packaging for a brand new laptop. And the brand new laptop was still in the box.

Normally, Gordon doesn't say much. He sits in the background, stupefied by his own brain power. Except when there's a brand new laptop in the room.

Gordon leapt on the box, ripped it open and started sniffing the polystyrene packaging as if it was infused with perfume or something.

'It's a Microcron Airweight 587X.SDR.' Gordon's voice slipped into a weird monotone as if someone had hypnotised him. I don't know what was in that polystyrene but it was having a weird effect on him.

'My bruv got a job lot. He's selling them cheap,' Freddo said. 'Something about the case not being quite up to standard.'

As you know I'm not very technically minded but even I was impressed with that laptop. It was no thicker than a thin crust pizza and the cool midnight blue case looked perfect to me.

Gordon stroked the Thin Crust laptop and sighed as he lifted the lid to reveal the keyboard. A silly smile broke out across his face and he went cross-eyed, as if he was in love.

Did I mention I always wanted a computer of my own? I was already thinking that maybe the Thin Crust laptop was too nice to use on a communication device. Maybe it would be more suitable coming with me back to Kepler 22b. It was small enough to fit in my rucksack and I reckoned I could persuade Freddo to give it to me as a leaving gift. But Gordon had other ideas. He whispered little snatches of baby talk and giggled coyly as he tiptoed his fingers over the keys. He was flirting with the laptop. *My* laptop.

I reached out and placed my palm firmly on the midnight blue lid.

Gordon snatched the laptop away and snapped it shut.

'It's not suitable for my device,' he said. His voice had gone all high and wobbly. I'd only ever heard him speak like that once before. When he was accused by Mr Pitdown of using the internet to find out information about the Egyptians rather than using a book like he'd told us to do. Gordon had been lying then and I suspected he was lying now.

'What do you mean?' I said. 'It's a keyboard, isn't it?'

'The wrong type of keyboard.' Gordon fixed his eyes on me. Only they weren't his normal eyes. Today's eyeballs bulged out of their sockets. Magnified by the thick lenses of his glasses, he looked totally freakish.

I'd never had a staring competition with Gordon

before. Normally his eyes are focused on his laptop screen, not staring me down like a demon. It was the most terrifying staring competition ever.

I didn't want to be ripped to shreds by Gordon the Demon, but I still needed to phone my fellow species on Kepler 22b and ask them to come and get me.

'What about the communication device?' I whispered without blinking.

'We'll use *my* laptop.' Gordon pushed his glasses back up his nose but didn't take his demon eyes off me.

'You mean the laptop you said we couldn't use?' I said.

'I'm prepared to make the sacrifice. I just need to transfer my stuff to this one.'

I reckon his eyelids were superglued open. The Geek didn't blink once. During this mission I've had my doubts about the level of commitment of my two best friends. But suddenly Gordon was serious. Deadly serious. I knew this mission was at an end if Gordon didn't get to keep the Thin Crust laptop.

But it was Freddo's bruv's laptop. What if Freddo said no?

Do you know what tension looks like? Me neither. But I felt it in the room right then. It was an invisible seething mass of darkness with crackles of electricity at the edges.

Gordon wanted the Thin Crust laptop for himself.

I wanted to use it to get me to Kepler 22b and maybe take it with me when I left.

I stared at Gordon's demon eyes for more than thirty seconds. I don't know what I was more afraid of: being stranded here on Earth or being stranded here on Earth with Gordon. In the end I decided Gordon could have the stupid laptop. I blinked and the staring match was over.

Gordon turned his bulbous eyes on Freddo.

Freddo's rubbish at staring competitions. He tends to get bored and thumps his opponent right between the eyes. It's cheating, of course, but his opponent is normally so busy nursing a bruised face that they don't bother arguing. But normally there's not a laptop at stake.

Gordon stared at Freddo.

Freddo stared at Gordon.

No one blinked.

I willed Gordon's eyeballs to stay in their sockets.

I willed Freddo's hands to stay by his side.

The tension grew darker, more dangerous.

After a couple of zillion years, Freddo spoke.

'Whatever!' he said and looked away. 'There's plenty more where that came from.'

Gordon the Geek pulled his eyeballs in and the tension fizzled to nothing. When tension disappears, it leaves a massive great 'What was that all about?' black hole.

The mission and our friendship had nearly been destroyed.

Gordon fumbled in his backpack for a load of cables and connected the two laptops together as if everything was business as usual.

I raised an eyebrow at Freddo. He raised both eyebrows in return. He can't do the one eyebrow thing. It's one of the things that differentiates me from humans. But it was good to share solidarity eyebrows with someone.

I was going to miss him when I was gone. But I wasn't sure I'd miss Gordon.

'The data transfer will take another seven minutes and fifty-six seconds,' Gordon said quite normally, as if he hadn't just reverted from being an eyeball-bulging demon. 'Where is the satellite? I need to work out how to reverse the polarity before I connect it up.'

It was good to get out of my bedroom. I left the

door open, hoping that the last shadow of tension would be gone by the time we got back. I led the way downstairs, ignoring the screaming coming from the kitchen, and out to the chasm of doom. It was even darker than normal but I could just make out the silver satellite dish in the gloom.

'That's no good,' Gordon said. 'A satellite dish needs to be fixed up high, if it's going to work. You know, near the roof or something.'

'Now you tell us,' Freddo said.

I couldn't speak because my teeth gnashed together uncontrollably. I'd faced death on that ladder for nothing.

'That would be the perfect spot.' Gordon pointed to the skinny bit of wall outside my parents' bedroom where the kidnapped satellite dish used to live.

I still couldn't speak. I turned to Freddo and raised my eyebrow again, only this time the eyebrow quivered uncontrollably.

'Okay,' he said. 'But you owe me.'

Freddo might have a few disgusting personal habits but he is the best mate anyone could wish for.

22

Communication - How To Do It

Jessie's wailing filled the whole house. Gordon and I crept past the kitchen door.

'I can't get it to work.' Mum sounded frazzled. 'Phone BT.'

'I could help them,' Gordon said.

'No! Not until we've sent our message to Kepler 22b.' We didn't have time to get involved with my sister's hysterics.

We were halfway up the stairs when Jessie screamed again. 'The phone's dead.'

'The phone and internet come in on the same wire,' Mum said. 'Pass me my mobile.'

I didn't bother hanging around to hear the rest of the conversation. I was beginning to wonder if that random wire lying dead on the pavement wasn't so random after all. I ushered Gordon upstairs and it wasn't long before Freddo joined us.

'Satellite dish in position,' he said. 'Ladder out of sight.'

I gave Freddo the thumbs up.

When Gordon is being geeky rather than freaky, he is very professional. It took him two minutes to connect his old laptop and the satellite dish (via a very long cable) to his communication device.

'What message do you want to send?' he asked.

My mind did what it always does when I'm asked a question under pressure. It turned stark white empty.

'Well, Mr Kendal?' Gordon put on his bored tone.

'S.O.S.?' I suggested.

'Are you in danger?'

'Not right now, but Jessie hasn't tried to switch on the TV yet.'

'How about . . . ?' Gordon started typing.

Kepler 22b.
Alien waiting for transfer.
Please collect from 26 Beechwood Road.

Gordon looked over at me and raised his eyebrows above the frame of his spectacles.

A few minutes ago he was going to kill me but now he gave me the solidarity eyebrows.

'What about all the other Beechwood Roads on the planet?' I said. 'I don't want them showing up at the wrong address. You better add the postcode.'

'And the country,' Freddo said. 'In case there is a Beechwood Road in Australia.'

Gordon made the changes, then pointed at the Enter key. He waggled his eyebrows at me.

For the first time ever, Gordon invited me to touch his laptop. I don't know if it was because he felt guilty about the whole demon eyeball thing or if he didn't care about his old keyboard now he'd moved onto the Thin Crust laptop.

I rubbed my finger clean on my jeans and pressed the Enter key.

The laptop screen sprung into life. Streams of writing scrolled up and off the screen. As the words sped past I could see some were in foreign languages. There were accents and umlauts all over the place.

Kepler 22b.
Alien auf die Übertragung warten.
Bitte sammeln Sie ab 26 Beechwood Road entfernt. CD47 6JT. Großbritannien.

Kepler 22b.
Alien bíða til flutnings.
Vinsamlegast safna frá 26. Beechwood Road.
CD47 6JT. Bretland.

Kepler 22b.
Alien oczekiwania na przeniesienie.
Należy zebrać od 26 Beechwood Road.
CD47 6JT. Zjednoczone Królestwo.

Kepler 22b.
Haole e kali ana no ka wehe 'ia'.
E'olu'olu, e ohi mai 26 Beechwood Road.
CD47 6JT. Aupuni Mōʻī Hui Pu 'ia.

ケプラー22bと。
転送のための外国人待ち。
26ビーチウッド・ロードから収集してください。CD47 6JT 。イギリス。

'What's happening? Where's my message gone?'

'Out there.' Gordon pointed through the window at the starlit sky. 'In every language known to man – German, Tagalog, Hawaiiaan, Japanese, Cantonese, Igbo, Swahili . . . I put your message through a universal translator. Once it's done the languages it will move onto Morse code, semaphore and pictograms.'

'Gordon, you're a genius!' Despite the memory of his bulging eyeballs, I wanted to kiss him. But with his hang-ups I didn't dare risk it. I gave him the thumbs up instead.

My message streamed up the laptop screen in languages I didn't recognise. He'd even translated it into Egyptian hieroglyphs.

'Bod?' Dad called up the stairs. 'Can you come down here a minute?'

Dad's voice seemed to come from a different world. A world I no longer belonged to.

'Daniel Kendal!' As soon as he switched to my real name I knew he was serious. I didn't want to leave the Supreme Communication Device but if Dad came upstairs he'd want to know why a cable was going into the front bedroom.

'Keep communicating as long as possible,' I said

to Gordon and Freddo. I dashed downstairs to re-join my human family.

'Have you got anything upstairs that might be dodgy?' Dad said. He had loads of wavy creases across his forehead, as if he was worried about something. 'I know that Freddo says that his family are strictly legit, but I want to double check.'

I didn't know whether communicating with an alien species was illegal but even if it was, I wasn't going to tell him about it.

'No,' I said.

'Has Fred brought anything round that might be stolen?'

Did he mean the Thin Crust laptop?

'Because I've called the police and I don't want to get Fred into trouble.'

'The police?' I said, trying to act innocent.

'Some idiot's stolen our satellite dish and they pulled down the telephone wire while they were at it. We have no TV, no phone and no internet. All communications are cut off, except for mobile phones.'

That wasn't strictly true.

Normally Dad would be impressed by Gordon's invention, but I couldn't share it with him right now. I'd tell him all about it when it was time to say goodbye.

A thick lump gripped me by the throat.

When I blasted off for Kepler 22b I'd leave everything behind. Everything and everyone.

'Dad, something's happening,' Jessie shouted.

We went into the sitting room to see what she was on about. Jessie stood in front of the TV with a remote control in each hand, zapping them furiously in turn at the TV.

'I had something just now,' she said as she zapped.

The TV screen buzzed with black and white fuzziness. The screen cleared and a stream of writing scrolled up endlessly. A stream of writing in every language on Earth.

'I think you should turn it off.' I leapt in front of the screen. I wasn't sure how good Jessie was at languages. She might recognise Beechwood Road in Afrikaans.

'Mind out of the way!' She shoved me just as the last line of foreign language disappeared off the top of the screen.

The TV started bleeping.

'-.- . .--. .-.. . .-. / ..--- ..--- -...'

That sort of thing.

‘Sounds like Morse code,’ Dad said.

‘Turn it off! Turn it off! I think it’s going to explode.’ I reached for the power button. In the moment before the screen blacked out a picture flashed onto the screen.

Gordon the Geek had left his web cam on.

Too Close For Comfort

'What was that?' Jessie zapped the remotes again and again.

'Just static,' I said.

'It wasn't static. It looked like a person.'

'You're hallucinating,' I said. 'You've got your friends on the brain so you imagined seeing them on screen.'

'I don't have any friends who look like that. But YOU do.' She jabbed the remote control into my chest.

'Kids, kids. Please. We're all having a bad day. Don't take it out on each other.' Dad took the remotes out of Jessie's hands. 'There's clearly a problem here, so let's calm down and find something else to do instead.'

'But, Dad . . .' Jessie said.

'But nothing.' Dad held up his palm. He didn't have to say, 'Speak to the hand,' Jessie knew what he meant. She didn't say anything but narrowed her eyes at me.

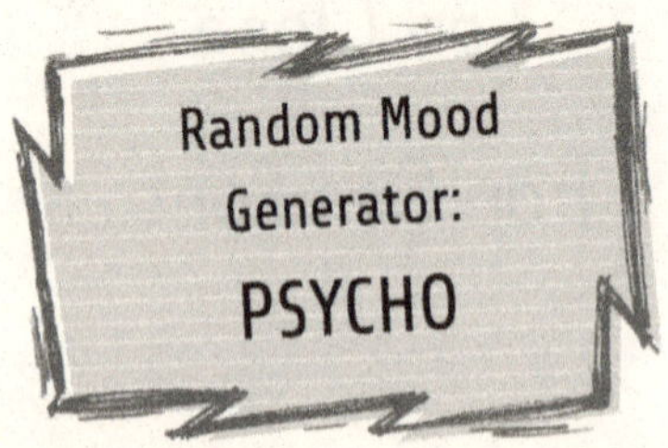

'I thought you said the satellite dish was missing.' Mum came into the room, her hands on her hips, weariness on her face.

'It is,' Dad said.

'Not any more,' Mum said.

Dad and Jessie followed Mum out to the front of the house. I legged it upstairs.

'They're onto us. Disconnect, quickly,' I said to my two friends, who sat mesmerised by the message scrolling up the screen on a continuous loop.

Gordon pulled out the wires and shoved his circuit board under the bed.

'I'm telling you. It wasn't there earlier,' Dad's voice came from the hallway.

'Well, it's there now.' Mum closed the front door. 'And I've just noticed, Timmy's playhouse has also been trashed. We'll have to put it back together in the morning.'

Freddo and I dashed into my parents' bedroom. Freddo reached out of the window and replaced Gordon's cable with the disconnected TV cable.

The message had been sent and the component parts of Gordon's communication device were all separated. Hopefully TV would be restored downstairs. The only problem was the dead phone wire. I couldn't do anything about that. I was sorry, but sometimes there are casualties on a mission.

'By the way, Dad says the police are on their way,' I said. 'That laptop's not stolen, is it?'

'No!' Freddo said. 'I don't think so. If it is, Dad's going to kill my bruv.'

He tried to grab the Thin Crust laptop but Gordon got to it first.

'Mine!' he said.

Freddo didn't bother arguing.

'Okay by me, Gordon my friend. You can explain where you got it from. I'm out of here, just in case. Dad says it's best not to be on first-name terms with the police.'

The doorbell rang.

Freddo threw open the window and was through it and shinning down the drainpipe before I could stop him.

'Are you going out that way?' I asked Gordon.

'I prefer to use the door,' he said.

'The police?'

'I haven't done anything wrong.'

'The laptop?'

'Freddo says it's not stolen.' Gordon shrugged. 'And they're looking for a satellite dish.'

Logical. Über-logical. That's Gordon!

'I'll see you out.' I went downstairs with him, just in case the police weren't quite so logical.

The Chosen One

I took a deep breath and opened the door, expecting to be arrested immediately. But it wasn't the police.

'It's him!' A woman with frizzy vermillion hair and long shabby clothes pointed at Gordon and threw herself at our feet. 'Take me with you!'

Gordon edged backwards as the woman pawed at his trainers.

'What are you on about?' I said.

'Kepler 22b. Take me with you.' The woman clasped her hands together in prayer. 'I beg you!'

'Seems like the message worked,' Gordon said.

I wasn't so sure. It was clear the message had gone somewhere. But had it reached Kepler 22b? The woman lying on our path didn't look tall enough to be a Keplerite. Her legs were too short.

'It's him! It's him!' Two more strangers ran towards us. One had grey, stringy hair and a shaggy grey beard. His hair was so long that somehow he had managed to knit the ends of it into a droopy jumper. A small woman skipped by his side. She wore a faded patchwork skirt and loads of brightly coloured beads around her neck.

'Get up, Myrtle,' the man said to the horizontal woman. 'Mind out so we can get closer to our saviour.'

Whatever I expected from sending the message to Kepler 22b, this wasn't it. These people clearly weren't aliens. They were too short for a start and if they had been adult Keplerites surely they would have worked out how to get back to Kepler 22b on their own by now.

'I think there's some mistake,' I said.

'No mistake! No mistake! This is 26 Beechwood Road, is it not?' The patchwork woman sang the words rather than speaking them. She skipped forward and twirled so that her beads swung out around her. She made me feel dizzy.

'Are you an alien?' I said.

'No, no, no!' The woman clasped her hands to her

WELCOME

mouth and crouched down in a huddle of quivering patchwork. 'I'm not worthy,' she said.

'We are the Returned,' the man said. He opened his arms wide and looked up at the night sky. 'The superior species returned us to Earth.'

'Heavens forgive us. We were not worthy,' Horizontal Myrtle said, tears in her eyes.

'I think we've got a case of alien abductees,' Gordon said, trying not to move his lips.

I thought we had a case of nutters.

'I don't get it,' I said out of the corner of my mouth.

'They've previously been abducted by aliens. Or think they have been,' Gordon said. 'They must have picked up our message and now they want to go back to Kepler 22b with you.'

No way! The Keplerites or some other alien species had rejected them. If they came with me, I might get mistaken for a Returner and be rejected as well.

A silver VW Campervan drew up on the other side of the road. It had blacked out windows and a satellite dish on the roof.

Beardie Jumper and Patchwork Woman snapped out of their dreamy trance.

'It's the others!' Patchwork Woman gasped.

'Quick, Myrtle!' Beardie Jumper shouted. 'I don't want the others getting the credit for finding the first alien on Earth. Grab him!'

Horizontal Myrtle lunged forward, her purple fingernails as sharp as talons.

'But I'm not an alien,' Gordon said, cowering from the hippy touch.

'We saw you,' Myrtle hissed. 'And so did the superior species. When they arrive, we will be waiting with you.'

'You've got it wrong,' Gordon said as he fixed his terrified eyes on me. The problem with phobias is they trump every other human emotion. Gordon didn't want these hairy hippies to touch him and I knew what he was going to say next. 'This is the right address, but I'm only visiting. A whole other family live here and he's one of them.'

I clapped my hand over his mouth, dragged him back into the house and slammed the door in Myrtle's hissing face.

When is a Friend Not a Friend?

'What did you do that for?' I shouted.

Gordon pulled out a disinfectant wipe and swiped it over his mouth. His neat freakery was driving me mad.

'I didn't know what to do,' he said.

'You were going to shop me to those nutters!' I said.

'They wanted to go to Kepler 22b with you.'

'Do you really think I want to go to Kepler 22b with *them*?'

The doorbell rang again.

'Are you going home or what?' I said. 'I think your friends are waiting for you outside. Not sure if you'll get home alive.'

'They are not my friends,' he said. 'Anyway, they want the real alien. They want you.'

'No!' I stabbed Gordon in the chest with an angry alien finger. 'They want the speccy geek who beamed his image across the airwaves along with my serious message.'

'Don't touch me!' Gordon said. He clutched his briefcase to his chest as he cowered away from me. 'I just want to go home and install all my software.

'Typical! Gordon didn't care if those weirdos ripped ME apart as long as no one touched HIM. He didn't care about anything except his crazy hang-ups and getting it on with his Thin Crust laptop.

Mum and Dad came into the hallway.

'Excuse me, boys. That'll be the police,' Dad said.

'Go and find something to eat in the kitchen,' Mum said. 'Then I'll run you home, Gordon. Bit worried those satellite thieves might still be around.'

Mum didn't realise that the real satellite thieves were now in the kitchen and were no longer friends. I couldn't forgive Gordon for trying to shop me to the nutjob Returners outside.

Gordon helped himself to a drink of water. He'd never drunk or eaten anything at my house before, he just wanted to look at something else other than me.

Jessie stormed in from the sitting room.

'Oh, it's you,' she said to Gordon. 'I saw you on TV earlier.'

'I think you may be mistaken,' Gordon said.

'I don't think so. Only it wasn't on any regular TV channel.'

'Is the TV working now?' I pushed my way between my incredibly annoying sister and my former second best friend, in case the traitor decided to shop me to my family.

'Yeah, only now Timmy is watching cartoons and I've missed *Hollyoaks*. Tragic, yeah?' Jessie flicked her hair away from her face.

'The omnibus is on Saturdays,' Gordon said.

'I'm not someone who catches up. I need to know what's happening right now. Got it?' Jessie pointed her finger rudely in Gordon's face. 'I'm going upstairs.'

'You have to ask permission to watch TV upstairs.' It was one of Mum's rules.

'I know,' she said. 'Where are Mum and Dad, anyway?'

'On the doorstep talking to . . . someone,' I said. I was going to say 'police' but if it had been them, Mum would have brought them in and made them a cup of tea. I figured Mum and Dad must still be out there trying to reason with the Returners. I gulped down a huge gob of guilt.

Jessie flounced out, drama queen style.

'Daniel!' she shouted two seconds later. 'Get out here. Quick!'

For once, the panic in her voice sounded real and as soon as I got into the hallway, I realised why.

The front door was wide open.

Mum and Dad were gone.

The Weird Case of the Missing Parents

How would you feel if your mum and dad disappeared two minutes after you had slammed the door in the face of a mad gang of alien abductees?

Pretty awful, right?

Well, I hope it never happens to you, because pretty awful doesn't cover it. I felt totally sick.

I ran out into the street hoping that Mum and Dad were having a chat with Mrs Fagan next door. I didn't care if Mrs Fagan told them that I'd been messing with the ladder and had brought down the telephone wire. *Anything* was better than Mum and Dad being kidnapped by Hairy Jumper and his mates. I didn't know whether they thought Mum and Dad were aliens like me or whether they just grabbed the nearest humans to take to show their fellow Returners. But there was no sign of Mum and Dad anywhere.

A muffled cry came from the motorhome parked opposite. It sounded like Mum.

'Hey!' I started across the road but the silver motorhome with sinister blacked-out windows pulled out and sped away.

'Mum! Dad!' I yelled but it was too late. The

motorhome turned the corner and disappeared.

The middle of Beechwood Road was the loneliest place in the universe right at that moment. Mum and Dad had been kidnapped and it was all my fault.

The VW Campervan spluttered into life behind me, Beardie Jumper at the wheel, Horizontal Myrtle and Patchwork Woman beside him.

'Where are they?' I leapt up onto the bumper and slammed my fists onto the windscreen.

'Mind out the way.' Horizontal Myrtle stuck her head out of the window. 'We are in pursuit. Our so-called leaders have taken the aliens to the rendezvous.'

The Returners had leaders. This wasn't just a random group of hippies. They were organised. They had plans. And right now those plans involved two totally innocent humans. Mum and Dad.

'Where are they taking them?'

'To higher ground, nearer the heavens. To be reunited with the superior species.' Horizontal Myrtle pointed a purple fingernail at the stars.

Beardie Jumper thumped the horn again and the van started moving. I leapt out the way before he ran me over. The ancient vehicle phutted its way down the street and disappeared round the corner.

'Will someone tell me what's going on?' Jessie demanded, her hands on her hips.

'Mum and Dad have been kidnapped,' I said.

'What?' she shrieked.

'By some alien abductees, who think your parents are aliens,' Gordon said.

Jessie opened her mouth to speak but instead of some sassy comment, for the first time in her life nothing came out. Nothing at all.

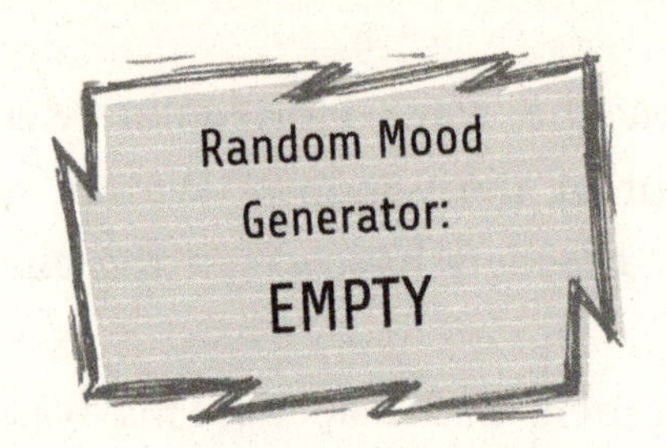

'We've got to rescue them,' I said.

'Alien abductees?' Jessie's mouth sprang into action again. 'This hasn't got anything to do with Serena Blake's gang, has it? They're called the Returners or something.'

'You know them?' I said.

'I know her. I told you, she's the craziest psycho in the whole of Year Nine.'

'Does she have a silver motorhome?'

'Her whole family live in motorhomes. Reckon they need to be ready in case they get the call from above.' She pointed to the sky.

'They think they got the call,' Gordon said.

'So where have they taken them?' Jessie said.

'Higher ground.' I shrugged. 'They think they're meeting an alien spaceship.'

'Park Hill Fields,' Gordon said. 'That's the only open space with altitude within a five-mile radius of this location.'

'I'll get my bike,' I said. 'Jess, you'll have to stay here with Timmy. Gordon and I will go after them.'

'No way. I'm not letting you anywhere near Serena Blake on your own,' Jessie said.

I was impressed. I hadn't realised she cared for me so much.

'And anyway, I want Dad back. He's supposed to be taking me and my mates to the Longitude Festival next week. We can't go without him. I'll ride Mum's bike with the child seat for Timmy. Where's your fat friend?'

'He's not fat. He just likes crisps,' I said. 'He's gone home.'

'Call him.' Jessie handed me her mobile phone. 'We need backup.'

Things were getting weirder by the second. I was allowed to use Jessie's mobile. She'd never even let me look at it before.

Two minutes later the Rescue Mission Team were ready to go.

Me on my bike, with Gordon perched on the luggage rack. Jessie on Mum's bike, with Timmy strapped safely in the child seat. He had a Lego model in his hands.

'He wouldn't leave it behind,' Jessie explained.

'And I don't want one of his tantrums.'

'*Vroom! Vroom!*' Timmy said and he whooshed his bunch of Lego bricks through the air as if it was an aeroplane.

Freddo zipped up the street on a mini motorbike. It sounded like a wasp in a hairdryer. Another of his brother's hand-me-downs. The bike was so small his knees came up to his ears, and he clasped the handlebars between his feet. I wasn't sure if it was a legal road vehicle, but I didn't care.

'Where are we going?' he said.

'Park Hill Fields,' I said.

'Follow me!' he said and buzzed off at full speed.

Voulez-vous Rendezvous?

Park Hill Fields wasn't far away but with Gordon on the back of my bike it felt like a million miles. It wouldn't have been so bad if he'd left his briefcase behind. It weighed a tonne.

When we arrived, I noticed the luggage rack was bent, but all I cared about was Mum and Dad.

Park Hill Fields does exactly what it says on the tin. It's a park, on a hill, with fields of grass. The only flat bit is right at the top. That's where the playground and tennis courts are.

The silver motorhome was parked right next to the swings. Its lights flashed on and off intermittently.

.- .-.. .. . -. / .-. . -. -.. . --.. ...- --- ..- ... / .--. --- .. -. -

'Morse code,' Gordon said.

'What's the message?' I said.

'We're nutters. Come and get us,' Freddo said.

Gordon squinted at the flashing lights.

'Alien rendezvous point,' he said.

'But Mum and Dad aren't aliens,' Jessie said.

'Unfortunately the Returners don't realise that,' I mumbled.

A stream of other campervans and mobile homes clogged up the road leading to the top and crowds of strange figures swarmed across the grass towards the Morse code message.

A lot of the Returners were hippies like Beardie Jumper and his friends, but some had made much more effort with their costumes. One group were dressed in black with yellow sashes across their

chests. They marched up the hill in an arrow formation. Another group had taken the Sci-Fi theme a little too far and were dressed as *Star Trek* characters.

'That's Spock.' Freddo pointed to a guy wearing plastic pointed ears and drawn-on Vulcan eyebrows. Spock was with the entire crew of the Starship *Enterprise,* including two Captain Kirks and a Lieutenant Uhura whose uniform was too small.

'That's Mr Pitdown,' Gordon said.

Sure enough it *was* Mr Pitdown, dressed as Dr Spock. Spock with a moustache.

'Moron!' Freddo and I said together, tugging at our invisible moustaches.

'How come you lot,' Jessie pointed at us, 'Know anything about that lot?' She pointed at the Returners.

'It was a mistake,' I said.

'Where's Mum?' Timmy's voice wobbled as if he was about to cry.

The massiveness of what I'd done sat like a huge boulder on the ground in front of us. Mum and Dad were now held prisoner, surrounded by a mass of deluded nutjobs. They *were* deluded, weren't they? Crazy, mixed up, confused. The Returners hadn't really been taken by aliens, had they?

And I guess that was when a question started forming in my own mind.

'I want Mum.' Timmy put his thumb in his mouth and started sucking furiously.

Poor Timmy! I reached out to hug him but Jessie got there first. Two big Timmy tears plopped onto her shoulder as she rocked him backwards and forwards. He was only a little kid. He needed his mum.

So did I. And our mum was here on Earth.

'Look, something's happening,' Freddo said.

A torch-lit procession marched across the hilltop and circled the playground. But these weren't battery powered torches. These ones had real flames.

Distraction Technique

The words 'burnt alive' came into my mind. I didn't want to say them aloud in case Timmy heard. I had no idea what these crazies were capable of, but I didn't want Mum and Dad anywhere near those flames. The human best friend telepathy must have been strong in the air that night because we all dumped our bikes in the bushes and ran up the hill.

Jessie told Timmy it was a race but she had to carry him most of the way as it was past his bedtime and his legs were tired. We didn't need to hide or sneak around. No one was interested in us. Every other person on that hillside was looking up.

The Returners had stuck the flaming torches in the ground. Beyond that circle, a ring of Returners held hands and stared up at the sky.

As more and more Returners arrived, they formed new circles, bigger circles, until the whole crowd was standing in rings facing the roundabout.

We stopped by the tennis courts to catch our breath.

A powerful spotlight swept across the night sky. It panned backwards and forwards, searching for the alien spaceship.

'Where do you think Mum and Dad are?' Jessie hissed so that Timmy couldn't hear her.

'There!' I pointed. A gang of Returners in silver suits dragged Mum and Dad out of the motorhome. Their hands were tied in front of them and they had white bandages wrapped around their mouths.

'What are they going to do with them?' I squeaked, my throat twisted in a hideous panic.

'Nothing, if I've got anything to do with it! That's Serena Blake!' Jessie pointed at a girl with a black helmet hairstyle. 'She's not messing with my family.'

'Wait!' Freddo grabbed her arm. 'There are too many of them.'

'We've got to do something,' Jessie said.

'We should give them what they want,' Gordon said.

'Which is?' Jessie asked.

'Dan,' Gordon said. 'He's the alien.'

'He's not an alien,' Jessie said.

'He is,' Gordon said. 'He wants to go back to Kepler 22b.'

'Shut up, Gordon! Shut up!' I shoved Gordon in the chest and he fell backwards onto his briefcase. 'Don't say another word.'

The whole Kepler 22b thing seemed totally stupid now. I didn't want to go there any more. I wasn't a nutter like the Returners and I wasn't an alien either. I wanted to stay here on Earth with my family and my friends, Freddo and . . .

Gordon looked up at me. His eyes swam with tears.

'I'm sorry,' he said. 'I thought you wanted to go

back to your family on Kepler 22b.'

'I've changed my mind, okay?' Angry spittle flew from my lips and splattered on Gordon's glasses. But the neat freak geek didn't clean it away. His shoulders heaved and big tears rolled down his cheeks.

And suddenly I realised he was telling the truth. Freddo hadn't believed I was an alien. He'd just come along for a laugh. But Gordon had taken me seriously. He'd totally believed that I was from Kepler 22b and had done everything possible to help me get back there.

But I wasn't an alien and the Returners had never been abducted by the superior species. In fact, there *was* no flipping superior species. I'm not even sure Kepler 22b could support life at all. Human or alien. It was just some theory put together by a bunch of scientists. My crazy mission had put Mum and Dad in danger and now I had been really mean to my second best friend who was only trying to help me. Gordon was stuck on the ground like a beetle on his back. I was the most horrible kid on Earth. No wonder I didn't have many friends.

'Don't be ridiculous. You're not an alien,' Jessie said. 'I was there when you were born. In Mum and

Dad's bedroom. Mum had you in the middle of the night. You might be odd but you're definitely human.'

'You said I was an alien. At breakfast the other day.' My voice sounded like it belonged to someone else. 'And there are no photos of me as a baby in Mum's album.'

'Yeah, I know,' Jessie said. 'Her camera broke before you were born. I broke it. Sorry about that.'

'And I found this.' I handed her the newspaper cutting about the meteor that was still in my pocket. 'It's about something coming to Earth from outer space on the day I was born.'

'Did it?' Jessie looked at the scrap of paper and screwed it up in a ball. 'Coincidence. You're a true Kendal, you know. You've got the Kendal tombstone tooth, haven't you?' She pulled down her lower lip. One big tooth stuck out in front of the others on the bottom row.

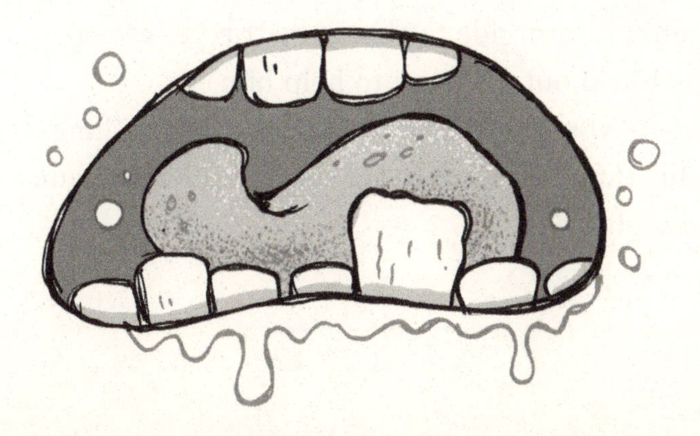

I pulled down my lower lip and rubbed my fingers over my teeth.

'That's genetics, that is,' Jessie said. 'DNA. You're my brother. A Kendal. A human.'

I nodded and turned away in case my tear ducts started leaking. Jessie was my sister. Timmy was my brother. Mum and Dad were . . . in danger.

'We've got to save them,' I said. 'I'm going to give myself up.'

'No way. I'm the eldest and right now I am responsible for you all,' Jessie said.

'It's not Dan they want anyway,' Freddo said. 'It's an alien spaceship. That's what they're looking for. Give them that and they will leave all of us alone.' He pointed to the spotlight in the sky.

Freddo might be a crisp addict, but today he was a genius like Gordon.

'Great!' Jessie said. 'Where are we going to get one of those on a Wednesday night?'

'I might be able to help you there.' Gordon rocked himself from side to side as he tried to get up.

I held out my hand to help him.

As you know, Gordon doesn't do touching. But this time he grabbed my hand and hauled himself upright.

'Sorry, Gordon. Sorry for pushing you. Sorry for everything,' I said.

'Thanks, Dan,' he said and he shook my hand politely. When he let go, he didn't rush off to get his disinfectant spray. I guess he'd forgiven me.

I don't know why he stuck by me when I was such a useless friend. I hadn't even written a message on his picture on the Wall of Wonders at school. I could have written *über-genius* or something. But his photo came down without a single comment.

Gordon had supplied the Cryogenic Practitioner's Secret Ingredient.

Gordon had suggested the sweet shop money-making scheme.

Gordon had built the Supreme Communication Device.

And now, Gordon reckoned he could supply an alien spacecraft to distract the Returners from killing Mum and Dad. He was a genius and a true friend.

'What do you need?' I asked.

The Alien Mother Ship

'What are you waiting for?' Jessie screamed. 'Look, they've tied Mum and Dad to the roundabout. If they spin that round, Mum will get all dizzy and throw up. She'll choke on her own vomit!'

'I need a camera, a laptop, a projector and something that looks like an alien spaceship,' Gordon said.

'Get real!' Jessie said.

But she didn't know Gordon the Geek like Freddo and I.

'You've got the laptop, yeah?' I said.

Gordon nodded.

'Can we use the camera on your phone?' I asked Jessie.

She thrust her phone into Gordon's hand. 'Try not to break it.'

Gordon selected the Thin Crust laptop from the collection in his bag and pulled out miles of cables. No wonder he'd bent the luggage rack on my bike – he was carrying the whole of PC World around with him.

'What's the plan, Gordon?'

'If I connect these two together and then run a cable into the back of the spotlight, I hope to be able to project an image of a spacecraft into the sky. We just need to take a photo of something that looks vaguely like a spaceship.'

Timmy held up his Lego model.

'*Vroom, vroom,*' he said.

'Timmy, you're a genius. But could you make it *zoom, zoom*?' I said. 'If you make a spaceship, Gordon can do a magic trick with it.'

Freddo and I left Gordon in charge of the techie stuff while Jessie and Timmy built an alien spaceship out of Lego.

The spotlight was mounted on a tripod. A huge industrial-sized thing that had to be dragged around behind a van. The spotlight was operated by a crew member from *Star Trek*. He sat holding

GORDON'S PLAN

the two huge handles and swept the beam of light across the sky and back again. Every time he changed direction the crowd hummed expectantly, but there was no spaceship in the sky and they were getting restless. If they didn't get what they wanted, they might turn on Mum and Dad and then anything could happen. We didn't have much time.

A ladder with a billion steps led to the top of the tripod.

My stomach clenched and I thought I was going to embarrass myself in my pants. I wish I'd never discovered vertigo. It had this nasty habit of taking over.

'We've got to get that guy down,' Freddo said.

Pre-vomit saliva filled my mouth. I didn't know what was more urgent: spitting it out or clenching my buttocks. In the end, I decided to do both.

Freddo must have realised I was in agony, so he chose that moment to stick the boot in.

'I don't know why you thought you were an alien in the first place,' he said.

'It seemed like a good idea at the time,' I said.

'And now?'

I shrugged.

Freddo raised his solidarity eyebrows and patted me on the back.

'How are we going to get rid of Mr *Star Trek*?' Freddo said.

'It's okay, he'll do as he's told,' I said. I'd seen every episode of *Star Trek* ever made and all the movies. The general crew never argue with the captain.

'Excuse me,' I shouted up.

The man ignored me.

'Hey, Trekkie!'

The man peered down.

'Captain Kirk wants you on the bridge,' I shouted.

The man nodded, climbed down the ladder and disappeared into the crowd.

Freddo climbed the ladder, the cable in his hand.

'You ready, Gordon?' I shouted over to the Geek.

He gave the thumbs up and Freddo inserted the plug into the socket.

The spotlight went out for a second and when it came on again, Timmy's Lego model hovered directly over the playground.

'*Vroom, vroom!*' my little brother shouted in delight. 'Big *vroom, vroom*.'

The crowd of returners went mental. The concentric circles surged forward as one, their circles becoming smaller and smaller at every step.

The flaming torches were out now but even if they had still been burning, their flames would not have stopped them. Every single Returner wanted to be on that Lego spacecraft. They moved towards the roundabout directly beneath Gordon's projection. The roundabout that Mum and Dad were tied to.

'Mum and Dad are going to be mashed in the crush!' Jessie screamed.

'Mum! Dad!' Timmy yelled and burst into tears.

'Move the spaceship!' I shouted up to Freddo. But he couldn't hear me over the cries of the nutjob Returners.

It didn't matter that I didn't like football or Mum had to look after Timmy all the time. I liked different things to them, but they were the only parents I had and I didn't want them to be crushed to death. I wasn't sure Freddo knew what danger Mum and Dad were in. I had to move that spotlight.

I gripped the hand rails on the ladder and took the first step. There was chaos all around me. People screaming, tripping over each other as they rushed to reach the alien spaceship, but I had to stay focused.

Step two. Step three. I climbed as quickly as I could before my brain could register what I was doing. I didn't look at the ground. I kept my eyes focused on the ladder rungs in front of my nose. My feet did the work, pushing me upwards. I did the rest, keeping my brain from telling me to be afraid.

The alien spaceship wasn't real. We'd put it there. It was an illusion. A bit like the danger of climbing a shortish ladder. I couldn't die from falling off this tripod, but Mum and Dad could die if those nutters trampled all over them.

I took the final two steps and hauled myself up. I grabbed the spotlight and swung it away from Freddo.

As the Lego spaceship moved across the sky, a cry of panic rose from the crowd. They must have thought it was leaving without them. Every single Returner on Park Hill Fields charged after it. Hippies, Trekkies and every other version of alien abductee broke ranks and stumbled down the hill towards the fake spaceship.

'Leave it hanging over school,' Freddo said.

'Never know, they might have to cancel lessons tomorrow if they get invaded.'

'Good idea! Now let's get Mum and Dad,' I said.

Freddo scrambled down the ladder first. The ground shimmered as I looked down but there was no way I was going to let a little bit of vertigo get in my way now. I jumped down after him and ran towards my lovely human parents.

Mum's terrified eyes softened when she saw us. I ripped the gag away from her mouth and fumbled to untie the industrial-sized cable ties at her wrists.

'Careful,' Freddo said. 'They're police-issue restraints. You might tighten them accidently. I'll show you how to release them. You okay, Mr Kendal?' Freddo helped Dad to his feet.

I led Mum away from the rendezvous point.

'Mum!' Timmy yelled and grabbed Mum round the knees. She lifted her handcuffed hands over his head and hugged him close.

'Hello, sweetheart,' she croaked and buried her face in his hair.

'Well done, kids,' Dad said. 'But will someone tell me what's going on?'

'I think it was a case of mistaken identity,' I said and hugged my average height, totally human dad.

30

The Problem With Police

It took us ages to get home. I suggested Mum and Dad should ride the bikes so that they could get home quickly but every time Mum tried to say goodbye, she became all emotional and grabbed the nearest child and sobbed into their hair. Or chest in my case. She couldn't reach my head.

'I think it would be prudent to stick together,' Gordon said, edging away from my overwrought mother. He was probably wondering how he'd get snot stains out of his blazer.

'I agree,' Dad said. 'We nearly lost you there. We thought we might be separated forever. I want all of you where I can see you.' He grabbed Jessie by the shoulders and me by the waist and pulled us in for a group hug. Freddo buzzed around us on his mini motorbike. Timmy sat in his bike seat while Mum pushed the bike along. Gordon trailed behind.

Police sirens wailed on the other side of town, over towards our school.

'Sounds like the whole police force are onto them,' Dad said.

'I guess we'll have to tell the police we were kidnapped,' Mum said wearily.

'If you do that, you'll have to go down to the station,' Freddo said.

'They might not believe that you are victims. They might think you are another group of Returners,' Gordon said. 'You could be arrested and locked up in the same cell as your kidnappers.'

'I don't want that!' Mum wailed. 'I just want to get home safely, and lock the door and forget all this happened.'

Dad didn't say anything but his deep worry lines were back.

I tried to send him a telepathic message. 'Don't call the police. Don't call the police.' I hoped Gordon and Freddo were doing the same thing. Telepathy is all about mates being in tune with each other and I think this time we were all thinking the same. We didn't want to explain ourselves to the police.

When we turned the corner into our road, a police car was already parked outside the house.

My stomach lurched and I had to go through the whole buttock clenching thing again. It wasn't vertigo this time, it was police-ophobia. I think I caught it from Freddo.

'I'm off.' Freddo slammed on the brakes of his motorbike. I guess he didn't want to show it to the police. 'Will you be all right now, Mr Kendal?'

'Sure, Fred. Thanks for your help.' Dad slapped him on the back.

'I'll head home as well,' Gordon said.

'See you tomorrow,' I called after them. 'If I'm not under arrest.'

My two best friends waved and made their way home together.

'Do you think you can convert my bike to methane?' I heard Freddo ask Gordon.

'Of course,' Gordon said. 'Methane is a form of natural gas. It is possible to convert a petrol combustion engine to run off gas.'

'Great.' Freddo stood up in the saddle and just before he turned the corner of the street I heard a sound. It might have been the motorbike backfiring but on the other hand it probably wasn't.

A police officer climbed out of his car as we reached the house. I felt pretty sick, I can tell you. Everything I'd done that day had been illegal one way or another.

'Did you report the theft of a satellite dish?' the police officer asked Dad.

'I did, but it's back now.' Dad pointed to the dish on the front wall.

'Wasting police time is a very serious matter,' the police officer said. 'Has your satellite dish been stolen or not?'

'No,' Dad said. 'Sorry, I was mistaken.'

The police officer didn't look very happy.

'There's something very dodgy going on tonight. The school's been invaded for an impromptu festival. You're not part of that, are you?' The police officer took out his notebook and looked us over suspiciously.

Dad might be unwilling to discuss how I came to be born but he'd never lie to the police. I decided it was safest if I answered the officer's question.

'We've been to the park,' I said. 'For a family game of football.'

The police officer eyed us up and down.

'Where's your ball, then?' he said.

'Some nutters dressed up from *Star Trek* stole it,' I said.

The police officer nodded wisely.

'Well, I think I better go and arrest them.' He closed his notebook. 'Shall I mark the case of the missing satellite dish as closed?'

'Yes, please,' Dad said. 'Sorry to waste your time, officer.'

'Good night.' The police officer nodded curtly and returned to his car.

'Thanks, Bod,' Dad said, when he'd gone. 'I thought we were going to be arrested.'

'Would you mind calling me Dan from now on?' I said.

'Of course, Dan.' Dad reached up and patted me on the shoulder.

'Let's get inside,' Mum said. 'No wonder the police officer thought we were with those weirdos. Just look at the state of us. Timmy in his pyjamas and your trousers halfway up your leg, Bod – I mean, Dan. You've grown again. I hadn't realised. We'll go on a special mother and son shopping trip at the weekend.'

'You're not going shopping without me!' Jessie said.

Mum looked at me, one solidarity eyebrow raised.

The Kendal family telepathy was working overtime. I knew exactly what she was thinking.

'Sure,' I said. 'Let's make it a family trip.'

'Speak to the hand, bro,' Jessie said, though this time she didn't shove her hand in my face. She held it up for a high-five.

I slapped it playfully away.

Mum and Dad exchanged one of their telepathically charged looks and they both smiled.

'Come on, Timmy, time for bed,' Mum said. 'I was thinking, Dan, would you mind swapping rooms with Timmy? There'd be more room for his train set and Lego. I thought we could get a loft bed and turn the smaller room into a teen bedroom for you.'

A loft bed at last! Mum was so relieved that we were all alive, she was in the mood to give me anything I asked for.

'Can I have my own laptop?' I said. 'I know where I can get a really good deal.'

'That's not fair! If he's having a computer, I'm having a computer!' Jessie said.

'We'll talk about it in the morning,' Dad said. 'Right now all I want is a cup of tea.' He ushered us into the house and shut the door, leaving the crazy world of Returners and aliens outside.

31

The True Meaning of Friendship

'Has your bruv got any more of those laptops?' I asked Freddo the next day at school.

'You won't need a laptop on Kepler 22b,' Freddo said.

'Different voltage,' Gordon said.

'The Kepler 22b mission is over.' I held my breath and waited for them to kill me.

'Thank goodness for that. Daniel Kendal has landed.' Freddo took a fistful of crisps and stuffed them in his mouth.

'Glad you're sticking around,' Gordon said but he didn't bother looking up from his laptop screen.

That was it!

They didn't mind that I had been a nutjob alien

for a while. They had forgiven me. Everything was back to normal. Freddo and his crisps. Gordon and his gadgets. Me and my mates. I let out my breath in one great big sigh.

I'm so lucky. I've got the two best friends on Earth.

Aliens – who needs them?

More HELP! adventures
– coming soon!

Help! I'm a Genius

Daniel isn't a genius like the rest of his family and he certainly isn't a brainiac like Gordon the Geek. So when there is a quiz to represent the school in a national competition he knows he will not be selected. However Daniel is wrong about most things, will he be right this time?

Help! I'm a Detective

Being the middle one in the family totally sucks. Daniel gets the blame for everything. A series of burglaries in the street gives him the perfect opportunity to prove himself. Once again he asks Freddo and Gordon the Geek for help, but are the three friends really cut out to be crimebusters?